# THE FASTING CURE

# THE FASTING CURE

By

**UPTON SINCLAIR**

AUTHOR OF "THE JUNGLE," ETC.

ISBN: 978-93-5128-544-1

First Published in 1911
Indian Reprint in 2017

*Published by*

Kalpaz Publications
C-30, Satyawati Nagar,
Delhi – 110052
E-mail: kalpaz@hotmail.com
Website: kalpazpublications.com
Ph.: +91-9212142040

**Cataloging in Publication Data—DK**
Courtesy: D.K. Agencies (P) Ltd. <docinfo@dkagencies.com>

**Sinclair, Upton,** 1878-1968**, author.**
The fasting cure / by Upton Sinclair.
pages cm
"First published in 1911"—Title page verso.
ISBN 9789351285441

1. Fasting. I. Title.

RM226.S56 2017 DDC 613.2 23

*TO BERNARR MACFADDEN*

*in cordial appreciation of his personality and teachings*

# Contents

# PREFACE

IN the *Cosmopolitan Magazine* for May, 1910, and in the *Contemporary Review* (London) for April, 1910, I published an article dealing with my experiences in fasting. I have written a great many magazine articles, but never one which attracted so much attention as this. The first day the magazine was on the news-stands, I received a telegram from a man in Washington who had begun to fast and wanted some advice; and thereafter I received ten or twenty letters a day from people who had questions to ask or experiences to narrate. At the date of writing eight months have passed, and the flood has not yet stopped. The editors of the *Cosmopolitan* also tell me that they have never received so many letters about an article in their experience. Still more significant was the number of reports which began to appear in the news columns of papers all over the country, telling of people who were fasting. From various sources I have received about fifty such clippings, and few but reported benefit to the faster.

As a consequence of this interest, I was asked by the *Cosmopolitan* to write another article, which appeared in the issue of February, 1911. The present volume is made up from these two articles, with the addition of some notes and comments, and some portions of articles contributed to the *Physical Culture* magazine, of the editorial staff of which I am a member. It was my intention at first to work this matter into a connected whole, but upon rereading the articles I decided that it would be better to publish them as they stood. The journalistic style has its advantages; and repetitions may perhaps be pardoned in the case of a topic which is so new to almost every one.

I have reproduced in the book several photographs of myself which appeared in the magazine articles. Ordinarily one does not print his picture in his own books; but when it comes to fasting there are many "doubting Thomases," and we are told that "seeing is believing." The two photographs of myself which appear as a frontispiece afford evidence of a really extraordinary physical recuperation; and the reader has my word for it that there was nothing in my way of life to account for it, except three fasts, of a total of thirty days.

There is one other matter to be referred to. Several years ago I published a book entitled "Good Health," written in collaboration with a friend. I could not express my own views fully in that book, and on certain points where I differed with my collaborator, I have come since to differ still more. The book contains a great deal of useful information; but later experience has convinced me that its views on the all-important subject of diet are erroneous. My present opinions I have given in this book. I am not saying this to apologize for an inconsistency, but to record a growth. In those days I believed something, because other people told me; to-day I know something else, because I have tried it upon myself.

My object in publishing this book is two-fold: first, to have something to which I can refer people, so that I will not have to answer half a dozen "fasting letters" every day for the rest of my life; and second, in the hope of attracting sufficient attention to the subject to interest some scientific men in making a real investigation of it. To-day we know certain facts about what is called "autointoxication"; we know them because Metchnikoff, Pawlow and others have made a thorough-going inquiry into the subject. I believe that the subject of fasting is one of just as great importance. I have stated facts in this book about myself; and I have quoted many letters which are genuine and beyond dispute. The cures which they record are altogether without precedent, I think. The reader will find in the course of the book (page 63) a tabulation of the results of 277 cases of fasting. In this number of desperate cases, there were only about half a dozen definite and unexplained failures reported. Surely it cannot be that medical men and scientists will continue for much longer to close their eyes to facts of such vital significance as this.

I do not pretend to be the discoverer of the fasting cure. The subject was discussed by Dr. E. H. Dewey in books which were published thirty or forty years ago. For the reader who cares to investigate further, I mention the following books, which I have read with interest and profit. I recommend them, although, needless to say, I do not agree with everything that is in them: "Fasting for the Cure of Disease," by Dr. L. B. Hazzard; "Perfect Health," by C. C. Haskell; "Fasting, Hydrotherapy and Exercise," by Bernarr Macfadden; "Fasting, Vitality and Nutrition," by Hereward Carrington. Also I will add that Mr. C. C. Haskell, of Norwich, Conn., conducts a correspondence-school dealing with the subject of fasting, and that fasting patients are taken charge of at Bernarr Macfadden's Healthatorium, 42d Street and Grand Boulevard, Chicago, Ill., and by Dr. Linda B. Hazzard, of Seattle, Washington.

# The Fasting Cure

## PERFECT HEALTH

PERFECT HEALTH!

Have you any conception of what the phrase means? Can you form any image of what would be your feeling if every organ in your body were functioning perfectly? Perhaps you can go back to some day in your youth, when you got up early in the morning and went for a walk, and the spirit of the sunrise got into your blood, and you walked faster, and took deep breaths, and laughed aloud for the sheer happiness of being alive in such a world of beauty. And now you are grown older — and what would you give for the secret of that glorious feeling? What would you say if you were told that you could bring it back and keep it, not only for mornings, but for afternoons and evenings, and not as something accidental and mysterious, but as something which you yourself have created, and of which you are completely master?

This is not an introduction to a new device in patent medicine advertising. I have nothing to sell, and no process patented. It is simply that for ten years I have been studying the ill health of myself and of the men and women around me. And I have found the cause and the remedy. I have not only found good health, but perfect health; I have found a new state of being, a new potentiality of life; a sense of lightness and cleanness and joyfulness, such as I did not know could exist in the human body. "I like to meet you on the street," said a friend the other day. "You walk as if it were such fun!"

I look about me in the world, and nearly everybody I know is sick. I could name one after another a hundred men and women, who are doing vital work for progress and carrying a cruel handicap of physical suffering. For instance, I am working for social justice, and I have comrades whose help is needed every hour, and they are ill! In one single week's newspapers last spring I read that one was dying of kidney trouble, that another was in hospital from nervous breakdown, and that a third was ill with ptomaine poisoning. And in my correspondence I am told that another of my dearest friends has only a year to live; that another heroic man is a nervous wreck, craving for death; and that a third is tortured by bilious headaches.[1] And there is not one of these people whom I could not cure if I had him alone for a couple of weeks; no one of them who would not in the end be walking down the street "as if it were such fun!"

I propose herein to tell the story of my discovery of health, and I shall not waste much time in apologizing for the intimate nature of the narrative. It is no pleasure for me to tell over the tale of my headaches or to discuss my unruly stomach. I cannot take any case but my own, because there is no case about which I can speak with such authority. To be sure, I might write about it in the abstract, and in veiled terms. But in that case the story would lose most of its convincingness, and so of its usefulness. I might tell it without signing my name to it. But there are a great many people who have read my books and will believe what I tell them, who would not take the trouble to read an article without a name. Mr. Horace Fletcher has set us all an example in this matter. He has written several volumes about his individual digestion, with the result that literally millions of people have been helped. In the same way I propose to put my case on record. The reader will find that it is a

[1] The first two of these, Edmond Kelly and Ben Hanford, have since died.

typical case, for I made about every mistake that a man could make, and tried every remedy, old and new, that anybody had to offer me.

I spent my boyhood in a well-to-do family, in which good eating was regarded as a social grace and the principal interest in life. We had a colored woman to prepare our food, and another to serve it. It was not considered fitting for children to drink liquor, but they had hot bread three times a day, and they were permitted to revel in fried chicken and rich gravies and pastries, fruit cake and candy and ice-cream. Every Sunday I would see my grandfather's table with a roast of beef at one end, and a couple of chickens at the other, and a cold ham at one side; at Christmas and Thanksgiving the energies of the whole establishment would be given up to the preparation of delicious foods. And later on, when I came to New York, I considered it necessary to have such food; even when I was a poor student, living on four dollars a week, I spent more than three of it on eatables.

I was an active and fairly healthy boy; at twenty I remember saying that I had not had a day's serious sickness in fourteen years. Then I wrote my first novel, working sixteen or eighteen hours a day for several months, camping out, and living mostly out of a frying-pan. At the end I found that I was seriously troubled with dyspepsia; and it was worse the next year, after the second book. I went to see a physician, who gave me some red liquid, which magically relieved the consequences of doing hard brain-work after eating. So I went on for a year or two more, and then I found that the artificially-digested food was not being eliminated from my system with sufficient regularity. So I went to another physician, who gave my malady another name, and gave me another medicine, and put off the time of reckoning a little while longer.

I have never in my life used tea or coffee, alcohol or tobacco; but for seven or eight years I worked under heavy pressure all the time, and ate very irregularly, and ate unwholesome food. So I began to have headaches once in a while, and to notice that I was abnormally sensitive to colds. I considered these maladies natural to mortals, and I would always attribute them to some specific accident. I would say, "I 've been knocking about down town all day"; or, "I was out in the hot sun"; or, "I lay on the damp ground." I found that if I sat in a draught for even a minute I was certain to "catch a cold." I found also that I had sore throat and tonsilitis once or twice every winter; also, now and then, the grippe. There were times when I did not sleep well; and as all this got worse, I would have to drop all my work and try to rest. The first time I did this a week or two was sufficient; but later on a month or two was necessary, and then several months.

The year I wrote "The Jungle" I had my first summer cold. It was haying time on a farm, and I thought it was a kind of hay-fever. I would sneeze for hours in perfect torment, and this lasted for a month, until I went away to the sea-shore. This happened again the next summer, and also another very painful experience; a nerve in a tooth died, and I had to wait three days for the pain to "localize," and then had the tooth drilled out, and staggered home, and was ill in bed for a week with chills and fever, and nausea and terrible headaches. I mention all these unpleasant details so that the reader may understand the state of wretchedness to which I had come. At the same time, also, I had a great deal of distressing illness in my family; my wife seldom had a week without suffering, and my little boy had pneumonia one winter, and croup the next, and whooping-cough in the summer, with the inevitable "colds" scattered in between.

After the Helicon Hall fire I realized that I was in a bad way, and for the two years following I gave a good part of my time to trying to find out how to preserve my health. I went to Battle Creek, and to Bermuda, and to the Adirondacks; I read the books of all the new investigators of the subject of hygiene, and tried out their theories religiously. I had discovered Horace Fletcher a couple of years before. Mr. Fletcher's idea is, in brief, to chew your food, and chew it thoroughly; to extract from each particle of food the maximum of nutriment, and to eat only as much as your system actually needs. This was a very wonderful idea to me, and I fell upon it with the greatest enthusiasm. All the physicians I had known were men who tried to cure me when I fell sick, but here was a man who was studying how to stay well. I have to find fault with Mr. Fletcher's system, and so I must make clear at the outset how much I owe to it. It set me upon the right track—it showed me the goal, even if it did not lead me to it. It made clear to me that all my various ailments were symptoms of one great trouble, the presence in my body of the poisons produced by superfluous and unassimilated food, and that in adjusting the quantity of food to the body's exact needs lay the secret of perfect health.

It was only in the working out of the theory that I fell down. Mr. Fletcher told me that "Nature" would be my guide, and that if only

I masticated thoroughly, instinct would select the foods. I found that, so far as my case was concerned, my "nature" was hopelessly perverted. I invariably preferred unwholesome foods — apple pie, and toast soaked in butter, and stewed fruit with quantities of cream and sugar. Nor did "Nature" kindly tell me when to stop, as she apparently does some other "Fletcherites"; no matter how much I chewed, if I ate all I wanted I ate too much. And when I realized this, and tried to stop it, I went, in my ignorance, to the other extreme, and lost fourteen pounds in as many days. Again, Mr. Fletcher taught me to remove all the "unchewable" parts of the food — the skins of fruit, etc. The result of this is there is nothing to stimulate the intestines, and the waste remains in the body for many days. Mr. Fletcher says this does not matter, and he appears to prove that it has not mattered in his case. But I found that it mattered very seriously in my case; it was not until I became a "Fletcherite" that my headaches became hopeless and that sluggish intestines became one of my chronic complaints.

I next read the books of Metchnikoff and Chittenden, who showed me just how my ailments came to be. The unassimilated food lies in the colon, and bacteria swarm in it, and the poisons they produce are absorbed into the system. I had bacteriological examinations made in my own case, and I found that when I was feeling well the number of these toxin-producing germs was about six billions to the ounce of intestinal contents; and when, a few days later, I had a headache, the number was a hundred and twenty billions. Here was my trouble under the microscope, so to speak.

These tests were made at the Battle Creek Sanitarium, where I went for a long stay. I tried their system of water cure, which I found a wonderful stimulant to the eliminative organs; but I discovered that, like all other stimulants, it leaves you in the end just where you were. My health was improved at the sanitarium, but a week after I left I was down with the grippe again.

I gave the next year of my life to trying to restore my health. I spent the winter in Bermuda and the summer in the Adirondacks, both of them famous health resorts, and during the entire time I lived an absolutely hygienic life. I did not work hard, and I did not worry, and I did not think about my health except when I had to. I lived in the open air all the time, and I gave most of the day to vigorous exercise — tennis, walking, boating and swimming. I mention this specifically, so that the reader may perceive that I had eliminated all other factors of ill-health, and appreciate to the full my statement that at the end of the year's time my general health was worse than ever before.

I was all right so long as I played tennis all day or climbed mountains. The trouble came when I settled down to do brain-work. And from this I saw perfectly clearly that I was over-eating; there was surplus food to be burned up, and when it was not burned up it poisoned me. But how was I to stop when I was hungry? I tried giving up all the things I liked and of which I ate most; but that did no good, because I had such a complacent appetite — I would immediately take to liking the other things! I thought that I had an abnormal appetite, the result of my early training; but how was I ever to get rid of it?

I must not give the impression that I was a conspicuously hearty eater. On the contrary, I ate far less than most people eat. But that was no consolation to me. I had wrecked myself by years of overwork, and so I was more sensitive. The other people were going to pieces by slow stages, I could see; but I was already in pieces.

So matters stood when I chanced to meet a lady, whose radiant complexion and extraordinary health were a matter of remark to everyone. I was surprised to hear that for ten or fifteen years, and until quite recently, she had been a bed-ridden invalid. She had lived the lonely existence of a pioneer's wife, and had raised a family under conditions of shocking ill-health. She had suffered from sciatica and acute rheumatism; from a chronic intestinal trouble which the doctors called "intermittent peritonitis"; from intense nervous weakness, melancholy, and chronic catarrh, causing deafness. And this was the woman who rode on horseback with me up Mount Hamilton, in California, a distance of twenty-eight miles, in one of the most terrific rain-storms I have ever witnessed! We had two untamed young horses, and only leather bits to control them with, and we were pounded and flung about for six mortal hours, which I shall never forget if I live to be a hundred. And this woman, when she took the ride, had not eaten a particle of food for four days previously!

That was the clue to her escape: she had cured herself by a fast. She had abstained from food for eight days, and all her troubles had fallen from her. Afterwards she had taken her eldest son, a senior at Stanford, and another friend of his, and fasted twelve days with them, and cured them of nervous dyspepsia. And then she had taken a woman friend, the wife of a Stanford professor, and cured her of rheumatism by a week's fast. I had heard of the fasting cure, but this was the first time I had met with it. I was too much burdened with work to try it just then, but I began to read up on the subject — the books of Dr. Dewey, Dr. Hazzard and Mr. Carrington. Coming home from California I got a sunstroke on the Gulf of Mexico, and spent a week in hospital at Key West, and that seemed to give the *coup de grace* to my long-suffering stomach. After another spell of hard work I found myself unable to digest corn-meal mush and milk; and so I was ready for a fast.

I began. The fast has become a commonplace to me now; but I will assume that it is as new and as startling to the reader as it was to myself at first, and will describe my sensations at length.

I was very hungry for the first day — the unwholesome, ravening sort of hunger that all dyspeptics know. I had a little hunger the second morning, and thereafter, to my very great astonishment, no hunger whatever — no more interest in food than if I had never known the taste of it. Previous to the fast I had had a headache every day for two or three weeks. It lasted through the first day and then disappeared — never to return. I felt very weak the second day, and a little dizzy on arising. I went out of doors and lay in the sun all day, reading; and the same for the third and fourth days — intense physical lassitude, but with great clearness of mind. After the fifth day I felt stronger, and walked a good deal, and I also began some writing. No phase of the experience surprised me more than the activity of my mind: I read and wrote more than I had dared to do for years before.

During the first four days I lost fifteen pounds in weight — something which, I have since learned, was a sign of the extremely poor state of my tissues. Thereafter I lost only two pounds in eight days — an equally unusual phenomenon. I slept well throughout the fast. About the middle of each day I would feel weak, but a massage and a cold shower would refresh me. Towards the end I began to find that in walking about I would grow tired in the legs, and as I did not wish to lie in bed I broke the fast after the twelfth day with some orange-juice.

I took the juice of a dozen oranges during two days, and then went on the milk diet, as recommended by Bernarr Macfadden. I took a glassful of warm milk every hour the first day, every three-quarters of an hour the next day, and finally every half-hour — or eight quarts a day. This is, of course, much more than can be assimilated, but the balance serves to flush the system out. The tissues are bathed in nutriment, and an extraordinary recuperation is experienced. In my own case I gained four and a half pounds in one day — the third — and gained a total of thirty-two pounds in twenty-four days.

My sensations on this milk diet were almost as interesting as on the fast. In the first place, there was an extraordinary sense of peace and calm, as if every weary nerve in the body were purring like a cat under a stove. Next there was the keenest activity of mind — I read and wrote incessantly. And, finally, there was a perfectly ravenous desire for physical work. In the old days I had walked long distances and climbed mountains, but always with reluctance and from a sense of compulsion. Now, after the cleaning-out of the fast, I would go into a gymnasium and do work which would literally have broken my back before, and I did it with intense enjoyment, and with amazing results. The muscles fairly leaped out upon my body; I suddenly discovered the possibility of becoming an athlete. I had always been lean and dyspeptic-looking, with what my friends called a "spiritual" expression; I now became as round as a butter-ball, and so brown and rosy in the face that I was a joke to all who saw me.

I had not taken what is called a "complete"

fast — that is, I had not waited until hunger returned. Therefore I began again. I intended only a short fast, but I found that hunger ceased again, and, much to my surprise, I had none of the former weakness. I took a cold bath and a vigorous rub twice a day; I walked four miles every morning, and did light gymnasium work, and with nothing save a slight tendency to chilliness to let me know that I was fasting. I lost nine pounds in eight days, and then went for a week longer on oranges and figs, and made up most of the weight on these.

I shall always remember with amusement the anxious caution with which I now began to taste the various foods which before had caused me trouble. Bananas, acid fruits, peanut butter — I tried them one by one, and then in combination, and so realized with a thrill of exultation that every trace of my old trouble was gone. Formerly I had had to lie down for an hour or two after meals; now I could do whatever I chose. Formerly I had been dependent upon all kinds of laxative preparations; now I forgot about them. I no longer had headaches. I went bareheaded in the rain, I sat in cold draughts of air, and was apparently immune to colds. And, above all, I had that marvellous, abounding energy, so that whenever I had a spare minute or two I would begin to stand on my head, or to "chin" myself, or do some other "stunt," from sheer exuberance of animal spirits.

For several months after this experience I lived upon a diet of raw foods exclusively — mainly nuts and fruits. I had been led to regard this as the natural diet for human beings; and I found that so long as I was leading an active life the results were most satisfactory. They were satisfactory also in the case of my wife, and still more so in the case of my little boy; the amount of work and bother thus saved in the household may be imagined. But when I came to settle down to a long period of hard and continuous writing, I found that I had not sufficient bodily energy to digest these raw foods. I resorted to fasting and milk alternately — and that is well enough for a time, but it proves a nervous strain in the end. Recently a friend called my attention to the late Dr. Salisbury's book, "The Relation of Alimentation to Disease." Dr. Salisbury recommends a diet of broiled beef and hot water as the solution of most of the problems of the human body; and it may be believed that I, who had been a rigid and enthusiastic vegetarian for three or four years, found this a startling idea. However, I make a specialty of keeping an open mind, and I set out to try the Salisbury system. I am sorry to have to say that it seems to be a good one; sorry, because the vegetarian way of life is so obviously the cleaner and more humane and more convenient. But it seems to me that I am able to do more work and harder work with my mind while eating beefsteaks than under any other *régime;* and while this continues to be the case there will be one less vegetarian in the world.

The fast is to me the key to eternal youth, the secret of perfect and permanent health. I would not take anything in all the world for my knowledge of it. It is Nature's safety-valve, an automatic protection against disease. I do not venture to assert that I am proof against virulent diseases, such as smallpox or typhoid. I know one ardent physical culturist, a physician, who takes typhoid germs at intervals in order to prove his immunity, but I should not care to go that far; it is enough for me to know that I am proof against all the common infections which plague us, and against all the "chronic" troubles. And I shall continue so just as long as I stand by my present resolve, which is to fast at the slightest hint of any symptom of ill-being — a cold or a headache, a feeling of depression, or a coated tongue, or a scratch on the finger which does not heal quickly.

Those who have made a study of the fast explain its miracles in the following way: Superfluous nutriment is taken into the system and ferments, and the body is filled with a greater quantity of poisonous matter than the organs of elimination can handle. The result is the clogging of these organs and of the blood-vessels — such is the meaning of headaches and rheumatism, arteriosclerosis, paralysis, apoplexy, Bright's disease, cirrhosis, etc. And by impairing the blood and lowering the vitality, this same condition prepares the system for infection — for "colds," or pneumonia, or tuberculosis, or any of the fevers. As soon as the fast begins, and the first hunger has been withstood, the secretions cease, and the whole assimilative system, which takes so much of the energies of the body, goes out of business. The body then begins a sort of house-cleaning, which must be helped by an enema and a bath daily, and, above all, by copious water-drinking. The tongue becomes coated, the breath and the perspiration offensive; and this continues until the diseased matter has been entirely cast out, when the tongue clears and hunger reasserts itself in unmistakable form.

The loss of weight during the fast is generally about a pound a day. The fat is used first, and after that the muscular tissue; true starvation begins only when the body has been reduced to the skeleton and the viscera. Fasts of forty and fifty days are now quite common — I have met several who have taken them.

Strange as it may seem, the fast is a cure for both emaciation and obesity. After a complete fast the body will come to its ideal weight. People who are very stout will not regain their weight; while people who are under weight may gain a pound or more a day for a month. There are two dangers to be feared in fasting. The first is that of fear. I do not say this as a jest. No one should begin to fast until he has read up on the subject and convinced himself that it is the thing to do; if possible he should have with him someone who has already had the experience. He should not have about him terrified aunts and cousins who will tell him that he looks like a corpse, that his pulse is below forty, and that his heart may stop beating in the night. I took a fast of three days out in California; on the third day I walked about fifteen miles, off and on, and, except that I was restless, I never felt better. And then in the evening I came home and read about the Messina earthquake, and how the relief ships arrived, and the wretched survivors crowded down to the water's edge and tore each other like wild beasts in their rage of hunger. The paper set forth, in horrified language, that some of them had been seventy-two hours without food. I, as I read, had also been seventy-two hours without food; and the difference was simply that they thought they were starving. And if at some crisis during a long fast, when you feel nervous and weak and doubting, some people with stronger wills than your own are able to arouse in you the terrors of the earthquake survivors, they can cause their most direful anticipations to be realized.

The other danger is in breaking the fast. A person breaking a long fast should regard himself as if he were liable to seizures of violent insanity. I know a man who fasted fifty days, and then ate half a dozen figs, and caused intestinal abrasions from which he lost a great deal of blood. I would dwell more upon this topic were it not for my discovery of the "milk diet." When you drink a glass of milk every half-hour you have no chance to get really hungry, and so you glide, as if by magic, from a condition of extreme emaciation to one of blooming rotundity. But very frequently the milk diet disagrees with people; and these have to break the fast with very small quantities of the simplest foods — fruit juices and meat broths for the first two or three days at least.

I will conclude this chapter by narrating the experiences of some other persons with the fasting cure. With the exception of one, the second case, they are all people whom I know personally, and who have told me their stories with their own lips.

First, I give the case of my wife. She has always been frail, and subject to sore throats since girlhood. In the past five years she has undergone three major surgical operations and had several serious illnesses besides. Two years ago she had a severe attack of appendicitis. The physician made a wrong diagnosis, and kept her alive for about ten days with morphine. She was then too low to risk an operation, and was not expected to live. It was several months before she was able to walk again, and she had never fully recovered from the experience. When she began the fast she was suffering from serious stomach trouble, loss of weight, and neurasthenia.

I did not think that she would be able to stand a fast. She had more trouble than I — some nervousness, headache and nausea. But she stood it for ten days, when her tongue cleared suddenly. She had lost twelve pounds, and she then gained twenty-two pounds in seventeen days. She then took another fast of six days with me, and with no more trouble than I experienced the second time — walking four miles every morning with me. She is now a picture of health, and is engaged in accumulating muscle with enthusiasm.

Second, a man well on in life, who had always abused his health. He suffered from asthma and dropsy, and was saturated with drugs. He had not been able to lie down for several years. He weighed over 220 pounds, and his legs were " like sacks of water, leaking continually." His kidneys had refused to act, and after his doctors had tried all the drugs they knew, he was told that he was dying. His brother, who narrated the circumstances to me, persuaded him not to eat the supper that was brought in to him, and so he lived through the night. He fasted seven days, and went for four weeks longer on a very light diet, and is now chopping wood and pitching hay upon his farm in Kentucky.

Third, a young physician, as a college boy a physical wreck from dissipation, now twenty-four. " A born neurastheniac." He was attacked by appendicitis twice in succession. He fasted five days after the last attack, and six days later on. Gained thirty-five pounds, and is a splendidly developed athlete; he runs five miles in 26 minutes 15 seconds, and rode a wheel 500 miles in seven days.

Fourth, a young lady, who had suffered a nervous collapse caused by overwork and worry. The bones of her spine had softened; her hipbones tilted upwards three-quarters of an inch;

she was "barely able to crawl on two sticks." She fasted ten days, and again eight days, and took the milk diet for six weeks. I have seen her every day for the last eight or ten weeks, and I do not think that I ever met a woman who impressed me as possessing more superabundant and radiant health.

Fifth, a young man, injured in a railroad wreck; a rib broken and the outer lining of the lungs punctured. Still has an opening for drainage, caused by chafing of the membranes. Suffered in succession attacks of bronchitis, typhoid, pneumonia and pleurisy. Was reduced from 186 to 119 pounds, and had planned to take his life. Fasted six days, gained twenty-seven pounds, and plays tennis vigorously, in spite of having an opening in his chest. Recently walked 442 miles in eleven days.

Sixth, a lady, married, and in middle life, a life-long sufferer from stomach trouble; had experienced six attacks of inflammatory rheumatism, resulting in valvular heart disease and the loss of the use of her limbs. Fasted four times — four, eight, twenty-eight, and fourteen days. I can best describe her present condition by saying that all this summer she arose every morning at daybreak, walked four and a half miles, went for a swim, and then walked home for breakfast.

Seventh, an Episcopal clergyman, who had suffered almost all his life from indigestion; had an acute attack of gastritis, followed by nervous prostration and complete breakdown. Specialists had diagnosed his case as "prolapsed stomach and bowels, autointoxication and neurasthenia," and told him that he could not expect to get well in less than five years. He was so emaciated that he could hardly creep around, and, despite the fact that he had a wife and six children, was contemplating suicide. He fasted eleven days, and then gained thirty pounds. I am prepared to testify that he is the most hard-working, cheerful and athletic clergyman it has ever been my fortune to meet.

I have taken some trouble to investigate the subject of the fast, and to meet people who have been through the experience. I could give a dozen more cases such as the above if space permitted. I know one man who reduced his weight from 365 pounds to 235. I know one little girl whose spine was bent in the shape of a letter U lying sideways, and who, by means of fasting and a diet of fruits exclusively, has come four inches nearer to straightness in a few months. She has the complexion of perfect health, and is rapidly recovering the use of arms and legs, which were paralyzed years ago.

The reader may think that my enthusiasm over the fasting cure is due to my imaginative temperament; I can only say that I have never yet met a person who has given the fast a fair trial who does not describe his experience in the same way. I have never heard of any harm resulting from it, save only in cases of tuberculosis, in which I have been told by one physician that people have lost weight and not regained it.

I regard the fast as Nature's own remedy for all other diseases. It is the only remedy which is based upon an understanding of the fundamental nature of disease. And I believe that when the glad tidings of its miracles have reached the people it will lead to the throwing of 90 per cent of our present *materia medica* into the waste-basket. This may be unwelcome to those physicians who are more concerned with their own income than they are with the health of their patients; but I personally have never met any such physicians, and so I most earnestly urge it upon medical men to investigate the extraordinary and almost incredible facts about the fasting cure.

. . . . . . .

Shortly after the above was completed the writer had another interesting experience with the fast. He had occasion to do some work which kept him indoors for a couple of weeks, under considerable strain; and after that to spend the greater part of a week in the dentist's chair suffering a good deal of pain; and finally to spend two days and nights in a railroad train. He arrived at his destination with every symptom of what long and painful experience has taught him to recognize as a severe attack of the "grippe." (The last attack laid him up in hospital for a week, and left him so reduced that he could hardly stand.) On this occasion he fasted, and although circumstances compelled him to be up and about during the entire time, every trace of ill-feeling had left him in two days. Having started, however, he continued the fast for twelve days. During this time he planned a play, and wrote two-thirds of it, and he has reason to think that it is as good work as he has ever done. It is worth noting that on the eighth day he was strong enough to "chin" himself six times in succession, though previous to the fasting treatment he had never in his life been able to do this more than once or twice.

## A Letter to the New York Times

(*unfit to print*)

Arden, Del., May 31, 1910.

Editor of the *Times*, New York City,

Dear Sir, — Some time ago your news columns contained a despatch to the effect that three young ladies in Garden City, Long Island, were undertaking a three days' fast as a result of reading a magazine article recommending this measure. In your editorial referring to this despatch, you say that the ladies are "the victims of a shallow and unscrupulous sensationalist." As I am the writer of the magazine article in question, I presume that this means me. I did not intend to make any reply to the remark, as I figure that I must have long ago lost whatever reputation could be taken from me by newspaper comments. Thinking the matter over, however, I concluded that I would venture a mild protest, not on my own account, but for the sake of the important discovery of which I told in the article in question.

It is one of the privileges incidental to owning a newspaper that one can call other people names with impunity, and can always have the last word in any argument. Will, however, your sense of fair play give me the privilege of asking you to state just what you meant by the slur in question? In the magazine article I stated that I had taken several fasts of ten or twelve days' duration, with the result of a complete making over of my health. I presume that the writer of the editorial had read the article before he condemned it. Am I to understand that he got from the article the impression that I was telling lies, and that I had never really taken the fasts as I said I had taken them? Or was it his idea that I exaggerated the benefits derived therefrom, in order to make "victims" of the three young ladies in Garden City?

I might say that I took the fasts in question in an institution where hundreds of people were fasting anywhere from three to fifty days; that during the entire time I was under the observation of many people; my weight was taken regularly every day, and all the symptoms which I described were observed by physicians and friends. May I also call attention to the fact that I published in the article two photographs, one of which was taken four years ago, and the other of which was taken after the fasting treatment? The contrast between these two photographs was sufficiently striking, it seems to me, to impress anyone. May I also call attention to the fact that the article was found of sufficient interest to be published in one of the most representative of the English monthlies, the *Contemporary Review*? Also that the *Contemporary Review* appended to the article the testimony of half a dozen people whose cases I had myself observed, and whose letters I have in my possession?

I fully recognize the fact that many of the things for which I stand as a writer are abhorrent to you, but surely that is no reason for condemning recklessly and blindly an important discovery concerning human health, simply because I happen to be the person who is telling about it. Setting aside all personalities, and simply in the interest of the discovery in question, I respectfully invite you to make an investigation of the claims which I have set forth in that article. Let me give you the names of some people who have fasted either under my direction or in my presence, and who will tell a representative of your paper of the results it has brought to them. I can tell you of a dozen such people. Also, perhaps by way of preliminary, you might be willing to publish as an appendix to this letter of mine the communication from another of my "victims," omitting the name of the writer unless you obtain permission to use it.

Yours truly,
UPTON SINCLAIR.

Appended to the above was the letter which the reader will find in the Appendix, page 111. The *Times* did not publish this letter, nor did it pay any attention to several letters of protest which followed. I leave it to the reader to judge whether the silence of the paper was one of dignity or of fear. The following despatch from the New York *World* of May 17, 1910, records the experiences of the Garden City ladies, and makes clear how much in need of sympathy my "victims" were.

All three of the young women are in rare spirits. They have gone about their usual occupations and recreations, and Mrs. Trask found time yesterday to talk about the single tax in the course of a conversation that had to do primarily with her newer interest.

"We are getting the most extraordinary number of letters about this adventure of ours," Mrs.

Trask said. "They began to come the first day, and to-day there were lots of them. They come from some of the most unexpected places and they contain some of the most unexpected things.

"What most astonishes me is that of all those who write to tell us that they have tried just what we are doing, not one has told us of a failure. There is n't any reason why they should n't write to say that we are foolish and that we can't hope to gain what we want, but dozens of them have reiterated the promise that we 'll never regret having made our experiment.

"One New York woman told us something that we had wondered about more than once. Her husband had suffered greatly from rheumatism, and finally he tried fasting. Not dieting like ourselves, but fasting. He went without food of any kind, she said, for nineteen days. He kept on at his work, too, which was the thing we had been wondering about.

"We 've heard from another physician, too. He lives in Boston and has made a specialty of dietetics. He warned us not to stick too closely to milk, because we 'd find that after a day or two it would quit being of the service it had been at first. People we never heard of tell us that thus and so was their experience, and when we measure our own discoveries beside theirs we find new and convincing evidence that we picked the true way to the end we hoped to reach.

"I know that for myself I 'll have reason to be grateful always that I took this up. We have been greatly benefited."

# SOME NOTES ON FASTING

In relation to the article, "Perfect Health," I received some six or eight hundred letters from people who either had fasted, or desired to fast and sought for further information. The letters showed a general uniformity which made clear to me that I had not been sufficiently explicit upon several important points.

The question most commonly asked was how long should one fast, and how one should judge of the time to stop. I personally have never taken a "complete fast," and so I hesitate in recommending this to any one. I have fasted twelve days on two occasions. In both cases I broke my fast because I found myself feeling weak and I wanted to be about a good deal. In neither case was I hungry, although hunger quickly returned. I was told by Bernarr Macfadden, and by some of his physicians, that they got their best results from fasts of this length. I would not advise a longer fast for any of the commoner ailments, such as stomach and intestinal trouble, headaches, constipation, colds and sore throat. Longer fasts, it seems to me, are for those who have really desperate ailments, such deeply-rooted chronic diseases as Bright's disease, cirrhosis of the liver, rheumatism and cancer.

Of course if a person has started on a fast and it is giving him no trouble, there is no reason why it should not be continued; but I do not in the least believe in a man's setting before himself the goal of a forty or fifty days' fast and making a "stunt" out of it. I do not think of the fast as a thing to be played with in that way. I do not believe in fasting for the fun of it, or out of curiosity. I do not advise people to fast who have nothing the matter with them, and I do not advise the fast as a periodical or habitual thing. A man who has to fast every now and then is like a person who should spend his time in sweeping rain water out of his house, instead of taking the trouble to repair his roof. If you have to fast every now and then, it is because the habits of your life are wrong, more especially because you are eating unwholesome foods. There were several people who wrote me asking about a fast, to whom my reply was that they should simply adopt a rational diet; that I believed their troubles would all disappear without the need of a fast.

Several people asked me if it would not be better

for them to eat very lightly instead of fasting, or to content themselves with fasts of two or three days at frequent intervals. My reply to that is that I find it very much harder to do that, because all the trouble in the fast occurs during the first two or three days. It is during those days that you are hungry, and if you begin to eat just when your hunger is ceasing, you have wasted all your efforts. In the same way, perhaps, it might be a good thing to eat very lightly of fruit, instead of taking an absolute fast — the only trouble is that I cannot do it. Again and again I have tried, but always with the same result: the light meals are just enough to keep me ravenously hungry, and inevitably I find myself eating more and more. And it does me no good to call myself names about this, I just do it, and keep on doing it; I have finally made up my mind that it is a fact of my nature. I used to try these "fruit fasts" under Dr. Kellogg's advice. I could live on nothing but fruit for several days, but I would get so weak that I could not stand up — far weaker than I have ever become on an out-and-out fast.

One should drink all the water he possibly can while fasting, only not taking too much at a time. I take a glass full every hour, at least; sometimes every half hour. It is a good plan to drink a great deal of water at the outset, whenever meal time comes around, and one thinks of the other folks beginning to eat. I drink the water cold, because it is less trouble, but if there is any hot water about, I prefer that. Hot water between meals is an immensely valuable suggestion which I owe to Dr. Salisbury.

One should take a bath every day while fasting. I prefer a warm bath followed by a cold shower. Also one should take a small enema. I find a pint of cool water sufficient. I received several letters from people who were greatly disturbed because of constipation during the fast. People apparently do not realize that while fasting there is very little to be eliminated from the body. (Of course, there are cases, especially of people who have suffered from long continued intestinal trouble, in which even after three or four weeks the enema continues to bring away quantities of dried and impacted fæces.)

Many of the questions asked dealt with the manner of breaking the fast; I suppose because I had been particular to warn my readers that this was the one danger point in the proceeding. I told of my experience with the milk diet, and I received many inquiries about this. My answer was to refer the writers to Bernarr Macfadden's pamphlet on the milk diet, as I took this diet under his direction and have nothing to add to his instructions. I might say, however, that I was never able to take the milk diet for any length of time but once, and that after my first twelve-day fast. After my second fast it seemed to go wrong with me, and I think the reason was that I did not begin it until a week after breaking the fast, having got along on orange juice and figs in the meantime. Also I tried on many occasions to take the milk diet after a short fast of three or four days, and always the milk has disagreed with me and poisoned me. I take this to mean that, in my own case, at any rate, so much milk can only be absorbed when the tissues are greatly reduced; and I have known others who have had the same experience.

While I was down in Alabama, I took a twelve-day fast, and at the end I was tempted by a delicious large Japanese persimmon, which had been eyeing me from the pantry shelf during the whole twelve days. I ate that persimmon — and I mention that it was thoroughly ripe; in spite of which fact it doubled me up with the most alarming cramp — and in consequence I do not recommend persimmons for fasters. I know a friend who had a similar experience from the juice of one orange; but he was a man with whom acid fruit has always disagreed. I know another man who broke his fast on a Hamburg steak; and this also is not to be recommended.

It has been my experience that immediately after a fast the stomach is very weak, and can easily be upset; also the peristaltic muscles are practically without power. It is, therefore, important to choose foods which are readily digested, and also to continue to take the enema daily until the muscles have been sufficiently built up to make a natural movement possible. The thing to do is to take orange juice or grape juice in small quantities for two or three days, and then go gradually upon the milk diet, beginning with half a glass of warm milk at a time. If the milk does not agree with you, you may begin carefully to add baked potatoes and rice and gruels and broths, if you must; but don't forget the enema.

People ask me in what diseases I recommend fasting. I recommend it for all diseases of which I have ever heard, with the exception of one in which I have heard of bad results — tuberculosis. Dr. Hazzard, in her book, reports a case of the cure of this disease, but Mr. Macfadden tells me that he has known of several cases of people who have lost their weight and have not regained it. There is one cure quoted in the appendix to this volume.

The diseases for which fasting is most obviously to be recommended are all those of the stomach and intestines, which any one can see are directly caused by the presence of fermenting and putrefying food in the system. Next come all those complaints which are caused by the poisons derived from these foods in the blood and the eliminative organs: such are headaches and rheumatism, liver and kidney troubles, and of course all skin diseases. Finally, there are the fevers and infectious diseases, which are caused by the invasion of the organism by foreign bacteria, which are enabled to secure a lodgment because of the weakened and impure condition of the blood-stream. Such are the "colds" and fevers. In these latter cases nature tries to save us, for there is immediately experienced a disinclination on the part of the sick person to take any sort of food; and there is no telling how many people have been hurried out of life in a few days or hours, because ignorant relatives, nurses and physicians have gathered at their bedside and implored them to eat. I can look back upon a time in my own experience when my wife was in the hospital with a slow fever; they would bring her up three square meals a day, consisting of lamb chops, poached eggs on toast, cooked vegetables, preserves and desserts; and the physician would stand by her bedside and say, in sepulchral tones, "If you do not eat, you will die!"

My friend, Mr. Arthur Brisbane, wrote me a gravely disapproving letter when he read that I was fasting. I had a long correspondence with him, at the end of which he acknowledged that there "might be something in it." "Even dogs fast when they are ill," he wrote; and I replied, "I look forward to the time when human beings may be as wise as dogs." I read the other day an amusing story of a man who made himself a reputation for curing the diseases of the pampered pets of our rich society ladies. They would bring him their overfed dogs, and he would shut them up in an old brick-kiln, with a tub of water, and leave them there to howl until they were hoarse. In addition to the water he would put in each cell a hunk of stale bread, a piece of bacon rind, and an old boot. He would go back at the end of a few days, and if the bread was eaten he would write to the fond owner that the dog's recovery was assured. He would go back in a few more days, and if the bacon rind was eaten would write that the dog was nearly well. And at the end of another week, he would go back, and if the old boot was eaten he would write to the owner that the dog was now completely restored to health.

Several people wrote me who were in the last stages of some desperate disease. Of course they had always been consulting with physicians, and the physicians had told them that my article was "pure nonsense"; and they would write me that they would like to try to fast, but that they were "too weak and too far gone to stand it." There is no greater delusion than that a person needs strength to fast. The weaker you are from disease, the more certain it is that you need to fast, the more certain it is that your body has not strength enough to digest the food you are taking into it. If you fast under those circumstances, you will grow not weaker, but stronger. In fact, my experience seems to indicate that the people who have the least trouble on the fast are the people who are most in need of it. The system which has been exhausted by the efforts to digest the foods that are piled into it, simply lies down with a sigh of relief and goes to sleep.

The fast is Nature's remedy for all diseases, and there are few exceptions to the rule. When you feel sick, fast. Do not wait until the next day, when you will feel stronger, nor till the next week, when you are going away into the country, but stop eating at once. Many of the people who wrote to me were victims of our system of wage slavery, who wrote me that they were ill, but could not get even a few days' release in which to fast. They wanted to know if they could fast and at the same time continue their work. Many can do this, especially if the work is of a clerical or routine sort. On my first fast I could not have done any work, because I was too weak. But on my second fast I could have done anything except very severe physical labor. I have one friend who fasted eight days for the first time, and who did all her own housework and put up several gallons of preserves on the last day. I have received letters from a couple of women who have fasted ten or twelve days, and have done all their own work. I know of one case of a young girl who fasted thirty-three days and worked all the time at a sanatorium, and on the twenty-fourth day she walked twenty miles.

## Fasting and the Doctors

A most discouraging circumstance to me was the attitude of physicians, as revealed in the correspondence that came to me. Mostly I learned of this attitude from the letters of patients who quoted their physicians to me. From the physicians themselves I heard practically nothing. We have some one hundred and forty thousand regularly graduated "medical men" in this country, and they are all of them presumably anxious to cure disease. It would seem that an experience such as mine, narrated over my own signature, and backed by references to other cases, would have awakened the interest of a good many of these professional men.

Out of the six or eight hundred letters that I have received, just two, so far as I can remember, were from physicians; and out of the hundreds of newspaper clippings which I received, not a single one was from any sort of medical journal. There was one physician, in an out-of-the-way town in Arkansas, who was really interested, and who asked me to let him print several thousand copies of the article in the form of a pamphlet, to be distributed among his patients. One single mind, among all the hundred and forty thousand, open to a new truth!

In the *English Review* for November, 1910, I find an article entitled "Bone-setting and the Profession, by Fairplay." It is a narrative of the experience of the writer and some of his friends with Osteopathy, being a defence of that method of treatment in cases of bruises and sprains. I quote the following paragraph:

"Harvey's statement about the circulation of the blood was met with scorn by the doctors, who called him in derision the 'Circulator.' Simpson's discovery of the use of chloroform was scouted by them as incredible, some even declared it to be 'impious,' and a 'defiance of the will of God.' Elliotson's use of the stethoscope called forth the rage of the protected society as a body: the *Lancet* described him as a 'pariah of the profession.' The ignorant scorn and slander broke his heart; but to-day the stethoscope is in constant use, and is recognized as one of the most important aids to a correct diagnosis."

It might also be of interest to quote the note which one finds appended to this remarkable article: "The Editor was amused to find that the *Lancet* refused the advertisement of the above article, thereby confirming what the writer alleges against the ring."

Of course I realize what a difficult matter it is for a medical man to face these facts about the fast. Sometimes it seems to me that we have no right to expect their help at all, and that we never will receive it. For we are asking them to destroy themselves, economically speaking. We do not expect aid from eminent corporation lawyers when we set out to overthrow the rule of privilege in our country; and it must be equally difficult for a hard-worked and not very highly paid physician to contemplate the triumph of an idea, which would leave no place for him in civilization. In an article contributed to *Physical Culture* magazine for January, 1910, I stated that in the course of my search for health I had paid to physicians, surgeons, druggists and sanatoriums not less than fifteen thousand dollars in the last six or eight years. In the last year, since I have learned about the fast, I have paid nothing at all; and the same thing is true, perhaps on a smaller scale, of every one who discovers the fasting cure. As one man, who wrote me a letter of enthusiastic gratitude, expresses it: "I have spent over five hundred dollars in the last ten years trying to get well on medicines. It cost me only thirty cents to use your method, and for that thirty cents I obtained relief a million-fold more beneficial than from five hundred dollars' worth of medicine."

Not so very long ago I saw a report in some metropolitan newspaper to the effect that the medical profession was greatly alarmed over the decrease in its revenues — it being estimated that the income of the average physician to-day was less than half of what it had been ten years ago. All this, I think, is directly attributable to the spread of knowledge concerning natural methods in the treatment of disease — and, more important yet, of natural methods in the preservation of health. Only the other day I was talking with a friend who was a teacher in a small college in the Middle West. There was a physician regularly employed to attend the girl-students, but several of the teachers became interested in the fasting cure, and whenever they learned of any illness they would go to the girl and start her on a fast; as a result, the physician lost considerably more than half his practice. In the same way, I myself recently started several people in a small town to fasting, and every time I saw the local physician driving by in his carriage I marvelled at the courtesy and cordiality he displayed; for before I had left that place I had cured half a dozen of his permanent customers — people to whom he had been dispensing pills and powders every few weeks for a dozen years.

# THE HUMORS OF FASTING

At the time of writing these words, it has been just six months since I published my first paper upon fasting, and I am still getting letters about it at the rate of half a dozen a day. The tent which I inhabit is rapidly becoming uninhabitable because of pasteboard boxes full of "fasting-letters"; and the store-keeper who is so good as to receive my telegrams over the 'phone, is growing quite expert at taking down the symptoms of adventurers who get started and want to know how to stop. I could make quite a postage-stamp collection from these letters — I had one from Spain and one from India and one from Argentina all in the same day. I am sure I might have kept a sanatorium for those people who have begged me to let them come and live near me while they were taking a fast. One woman writes to ask me to name my own price to take charge of a case of elephantiasis which has been given up by all the experts in Europe!

Also, I could fill an article with the "humors" of these letters. One woman writes a long and anxious inquiry as to whether it is permissible to drink any *water* while fasting; and then follows this up with a special delivery letter to say that she hopes I will not think she is crazy — she had read the article again and noted the injunction to drink as much water as she can! And then comes a letter from a man who wants to know if I really mean it all; do I truly expect him to eat nothing whatever — or would I call it fasting if he ate just nuts and fruit now and then? Quite recently I was talking with a physician — a successful and well-known physician — who refused point-blank to believe that a human being could live for more than four or five days without any sort of nutriment. There was no use talking about it — it was a physiological impossibility; and even when I offered him the names and addresses of a hundred people who had done it, he went off unconvinced. And yet that same physician professes a religion which through nearly two thousand years has recommended "fasting and prayer" as the method of the soul's achievement; and he will go to church and listen reverently to accounts of a forty-day fast in the wilderness! And he lives in a country in which there are sanatoriums where hundreds of people are fasting all the time, and where twenty or thirty-day fasts occasion no more remark than a good golf-score at a summer hotel!

If you have any doubt that such fasts are taken, you can very quickly convince yourself. Less than a year ago I saw a man completing a fifty-day fast; I talked with him day by day, and I knew absolutely that it was all in good faith. The symptoms of fasting are as distinct and unmistakable as are, for instance, those of small-pox; you could no more persuade an experienced person that you are fasting when you are not fasting, than you could persuade a bacteriologist that you had sleeping-sickness when you were merely lazy.

When I was a very small boy, I recall that a Dr. Tanner took a forty-day fast in a museum in New York; and I recollect well the conversation in our family — how obvious it was that the thing must be a fake, and how foolish people were to be taken in by so absurd a fake. "He gets something to eat when nobody 's looking," we would say.

But then what about his weight? Here is a man, going along day by day, year in and year out, weighing in the neighborhood of a hundred and fifty pounds; and now, all of a sudden, he begins to lose a pound a day, as regularly as the sun rises. How does he do it?

"Well," we would say, "he must work hard and get rid of it."

But how can a man do that, when he had no longer enough muscular tissue left to support his weight? And when his pulse is only thirty-five beats to the minute?

Then, says the reader, perhaps he goes to a Turkish bath, and sweats it off.

But ask any jockey how he 'd like to take a Turkish bath every day for fifty days! And how he would stand it when his arms and thighs were so reduced that you could meet your thumb and forefinger around them, and could plainly trace the bones and the blood vessels! And then again, there is the tongue. If you take a fast and really need the fast, you will find your tongue so coated that you can scrape it with a knife-blade. And if you break your fast, your tongue will clear in twenty-four hours; nothing in the world will coat it again but several days more of fasting. How would you propose to get around that difficulty?

Such ideas have to do with fasting as seen by the outsider. I recollect reading a diverting account of the fasting cure, in which the victim was portrayed as haunted by the ghost of beef-steaks and turkeys. But the person who is taking the fast knows nothing of these troubles, nor would there be much profit in fasting if he did. The fast is not an ordeal, it is a rest; and I have known people to lose interest in food as completely as if they had never tasted any in their lives. I know one lady who, to the consternation of her friends and relatives, began a fast three days before Christmas and continued it until three days after New Year's; and on both the holidays she cooked a turkey and served it for her children. On another occasion, during a week's fast, she "put up" several gallons of preserves; the only inconvenience being that she had to call in a neighbor to taste them and see if they were done. I myself took a twelve-day fast while living alone with my little boy, and three times every day I went into the pantry and set out a meal for him. I was not troubled at all by the sight of the food.

The longest fast of which I had heard when my article was written was seventy-eight days; but that record has since been broken, by a man named Richard Fausel. Mr. Fausel, who keeps a hotel somewhere in North Dakota, had presumably partaken too generously of the good cheer intended for his guests, for he found himself at the inconvenient weight of three hundred and eighty-five pounds. He went to a sanatorium in Battle Creek and there fasted for forty days (if my recollection serves me), and by dint of vigorous exercise meanwhile, he got rid of one hundred and thirty pounds. I think I never saw a funnier sight than Mr. Fausel at the conclusion of this fast, wearing the same pair of trousers that he had worn at the beginning of it. But the temptations of hotel-keeping are severe, and when he went back home, he found himself going up in weight again. This time he concluded to do the job thoroughly, and went to Macfadden's place in Chicago, and set out upon a fast of ninety days. That is a new record — though I sometimes wonder if it is quite fair to call it "fasting" when a man is simply living upon an internal larder of fat.

It must be a curious experience to go for three months without tasting food. It is no wonder that the stomach and all the organs of assimilation forget how to do their work. The one danger in the fasting treatment is that when you break the fast, hunger is apt to come back with a rush, while, on the other hand, the stomach is weak, and the utmost caution is needed. If you yield to your cravings, you may fill your whole system with toxins, and undo all the good of the treatment; but if you go slowly, and restrict yourself to very small quantities of the most easily assimilated foods, then in an incredibly short time the body will have regained its strength.

My experience has taught me that it is well not to be too proud at such a time, but to get some one to help you. And it ought to be some one who has fasted, for a person at the end of a fast is an agitating sight to his neighbors, and their one impulse is to get a "square meal" into him as quickly as possible. Quite recently there was one of my converts camping on my trail in New York City, and he called at the home of a relative of mine, an elderly lady, who does not take much stock in my eccentricities. I shall not soon forget her description of his appearance — "I thought he was going to die right there before my eyes!" she said. And no wonder, since the poor fellow had climbed four flights of stairs to the apartment. "I know you 'll get into trouble," added my relative, "if you don't stop advising people to do such things!"

I was interested enough in the question of fasting to spend some time at a sanatorium where they make a specialty of it. One can see a sicker looking collection of humans in such a place than anywhere else in the world, I fancy. In the first place, people do not take the fasting cure until they are looking desperate; and when they have got into the fast they look more desperate. At the later stages they sometimes take to wheelchairs; and at all times they move with deliberation, and their faces wear serious expressions. They gather in little groups and discuss their symptoms; there is nothing so interesting in the world when you are fasting as to talk symptoms with a lot of people who are doing the same thing. There are some who are several days ahead of you, and who make you ashamed of your doubts; and others who are behind you, and to whom you have to appear as an old campaigner. So you develop an *esprit de corps,* as it were — though that sounds as if I were trying to make a pun.

All this may not seem very alluring; but it is far better than a life-time of illness, such as many of these people have known before. I never knew that there was such terrible suffering in the world until I heard some of their stories; they would indeed be depressing company, were it not for the fact that now they are getting well. The reader may answer sarcastically that they *think* they are. But every Christian Scientist knows that this comes to the same thing; and I have talked with not less than a hundred people who have fasted for three days or more, and out of these there were but two or three who did not report themselves as greatly benefited. So I am accustomed to say that I would rather spend my time in a fasting sanatorium than in an ordinary "swell" hotel. The people in the former are making themselves well and know it; while the people in the latter are making themselves ill, and don't know it.

## A SYMPOSIUM ON FASTING

RECENTLY I published a request that those who had tried the fast as the result of my advocacy would write to advise me of the results. I stated that I desired to hear unfavorable results as well as favorable; that I wanted to get at the facts, and would tabulate the results exactly as they came. The questions asked were as follows:

1. How many times have you fasted?
2. How many days on each occasion?
3. From what complaints did you suffer?
4. Were these complaints ever diagnosed by regular physician? If so, give the names and addresses of these physicians.
5. Do you consider that you were definitely benefited by the fasts? If so, in what way?
6. For how long did the benefit continue?
7. Do you consider that you were completely cured?
8. Do you consider that you were definitely harmed? If so, in what way?
9. Have you ever been examined by any regular physician since the cure? If so, give name and address.

10. Are you willing that your name and address should be quoted for the benefit of others?

The total number of fasts taken was 277, and the average number of days was 6. There were 90 of five days or over, 51 of ten days or over, and 6 of 30 days or over. Out of the 109 persons who wrote to me, 100 reported benefit, and 17 no benefit. Of these 17 about half give wrong breaking of the fast as the reason for the failure. In cases where the cure had not proved permanent, about half mentioned that the recurrence of the trouble was caused by wrong eating, and about half of the rest made this quite evident by what they said. Also it is to be noted that in the cases of the 17 who got no benefit, nearly all were fasts of only three or four days.

Following is the complete list of diseases benefited — 45 of the cases having been diagnosed by physicians: indigestion (usually associated with nervousness), 27; rheumatism, 5; colds, 8; tuberculosis, 4; constipation, 14; poor circulation, 3; headaches, 5; anæmia, 3; scrofula, 1; bronchial trouble, 5; syphilis, 1; liver trouble, 5; general debility, 5; chills and fever, 1; blood poisoning, 1; ulcerated leg, 1; neurasthenia, 6; locomotor ataxia, 1; sciatica, 1; asthma, 2; excess of uric acid, 1; epilepsy, 1; pleurisy, 1; impaction of bowels, 1; eczema, 2; catarrh, 6; appendicitis, 3; valvular disease of heart, 1; insomnia, 1; gas poisoning, 1; grippe, 1; cancer, 1.

There follows a brief summary of some of the most interesting cases. A number of longer letters will be found in the Appendix.

Mrs. Lulu Wallace Smith, 324 W. White Oak Ave., Monrovia, Cal. Age 28. Fasted 30 days for appendicitis and peritonitis, diagnosed by four physicians. "Yes, indeed, I have definitely been benefited by fasting. My stomach is not distressed after meals, I have regular evacuations of the intestines, which I had not had since I was seventeen. I feel perfectly healthy and look the same."

William N——. Syphilis, with advanced ulcers in throat. Physicians declared the case hopeless. Complete disappearance of symptoms after four day's fast, but they gradually reappeared, and longer fast intended.

Dora Jordan, Connersville, Md. Indigestion, extreme nervousness, neuralgia in its worst form. Fasted thirty days; did most of cooking for a family of five, was at no time tempted to eat. "I am no longer troubled with the old diseases, and weigh more than ever before. After my fast I felt as happy and care free as a little child."

C. L. Clark, Greenville, Mich. Nervous, poor digestion. Fasted nine days. "I have been wonderfully benefited, and am a rabid convert. Alas, for the poor mortal who shows the faintest spark of interest in my fast — I hand him the whole works, lock, stock and barrel! I feel a new power and new incentive in life. Whenever I see a sick person, I feel like telling him that for all he knows to the contrary, good health has been and may be only eight or ten days away and waiting for years for him to claim it."

T. S. Jacks, Muskegon, Mich. Twenty days, followed by shorter fasts, for stomach trouble, diagnosed by Dr. M—— as cancer. "He advised me to be operated on. Since my fast, three years ago, I have had no trouble with my stomach. I am entirely cured, and am enjoying fine health."

Gordon G. Ives, 147 Forsythe Bldg., Fresno, Cal. "Have fasted a good many times since 1899, to cure catarrh of stomach, constipation, deafness of four months' standing, neuralgia, etc. Duration, from one to sixteen days. Never failed in accomplishing a cure. Benefit continued until I had over-eaten for a long time. Complaints were never diagnosed by regular physicians, as I got on to them in 1894. Use my name if it will help the truth."

Mrs. Maria L. Scott, Boring, Ariz. Reports case of husband, who fasted seven days for constipation and deafness; had been obliged to take enema daily for several months. Complete cure.

Mrs. A. Wears, De Funiak Springs, Fla. "Age forty-two, subject to severe colds and sore throat all my life, chronic catarrh of head and throat, in bed two winters with bronchitis and asthma. Did not take complete fast. My catarrh is much improved. I feel perfectly well and enjoy life so much more than I did before the fast."

Mrs. Mae Bramble, Alba, Pa., R. F. D. 70. One fast of thirty days, another of three days; nervous prostration the first time, appendicitis the second time. "The first complaint was diagnosed, the second was not; as I am a professional nurse, I understood the symptoms myself." Complete and permanent cure. "I have never had a return of the nervous trouble, and am well of the other complaint. It is five years since the first fast."

M. E. Beard, Corning, Cal. Fasted nine days for scrofula. Had been diagnosed. Complete cure, permanent since 1908. Age forty-seven. "Five years ago I broke down. Physicians never could tell me what ailed me. I kept busy during my fast physically and mentally; worked over the cook stove and outdoors. Felt no weakness."

Joseph L. Lewis, Hatfield, Ark. Fasted three days, and then four days. "During the last ten days have felt better than at any time during the last seven years."

Monroe Bornn, Port of Spain, Trinidad. Fasted seven days on three occasions, for liver trouble. "I had been treated by three physicians. I consider that I was completely cured. I have been examined by regular physicians since the cure."

E. B. Bayne, White Plains, N. Y. Sends record of fasts taken by two people, Mr. and Mrs. A. Mr. A. fasted for rheumatism, which had caused kidney and bladder trouble of years' standing, and iritis; fasted five days and then four days and was completely cured. Mrs. A. Neuralgia and catarrhal deafness. Completely cured. "Finds that exposure to draughts has no effect upon her whatever, heretofore she would catch cold upon the least exposure."

Mrs. Charles H. Vosseller, Newark, N. J. "I don't agree with you or Bernarr Macfadden in not recommending fasting for tuberculosis. My case was diagnosed by Dr. B. G——, New Brunswick, N. J. I fasted nineteen days and was completely cured; I received no harm, and have been examined since by a physician. I weigh 114 lbs. now and before my fast weighed 100 lbs. I never felt better in my life than I do at present. Do not know that I have a pair of lungs."

In connection with the above tabulation of results, it should be specified that it does not include any of the cases quoted elsewhere in the book; it includes some of the letters given in the Appendix, but not all. Thus it will appear that there are many more than 277 cases of fasting recorded in this volume. The reason that I did not summarize in the tabulation all the letters I have received is, that I wished to give only those which were sent to me in answer to my definite series of questions, so that I might be sure of getting the unfavorable as well as the favorable reports. Recently a well-known physician who edits a magazine of health came out in vehement opposition to the fasting cure, maintaining that we hear only of the cases which are successful, and do not hear of the disastrous failures. In reply to this, I wrote to him suggesting that he publish my series of questions in his magazine, thus giving his readers an opportunity to make me acquainted with the unsuccessful cases. This, however, the physician declined to do.

## Death during the Fast

There was much newspaper discussion of my fasting papers — most of it being sarcastic. The most biting comment that I recall came from somewhere out West, and ran about as follows: "A Seattle man fasted forty days for stomach trouble. His stomach is troubling him no longer. He is dead." I set to work to find out about this case, and I give the facts on page 137. I also saw a report from the London *Daily Telegraph* to the effect that a man had died in South

Africa as a result of trying my "cure." How many thousands of people tried it and lived, I do not know; but horrified relatives and enterprising newspaper writers would see that the public was informed about any that died.

As to the possibility or probability of death during a fast, I have one or two points to note:

First, a good many sick people are dying all the time. It would be an argument for fasting if it saved any of them. It is no argument against fasting that it fails to save them all. No one would think of bringing it up against his surgeon or his family physician that he occasionally lost a patient.

Second, people might die very frequently, without that being an argument against the cure. It might simply be a consequence of the desperately ill class of people who were trying it. A doctor who had a new method of healing, and was permitted to use it only upon those whom all other doctors had given up, would be considered successful if he effected even an occasional cure. I would wager that of the people who read my article and set out to fast, practically all had been suffering for many years, and had given the "regular" physicians unlimited opportunity to work on them.

Third, it may be set down as absolutely certain

that no one ever died of starvation while fasting. The essential feature of the fast is that after the first two or three days all hunger ceases; and that any one could die of lack of food without feeling a desire for food, is absurd upon the face of it. Nature simply does not work that way. It reminds me of a young lady who once told me that she would not go to sleep with a mouse in the room, because she imagined the mouse might nibble off her ear without waking her!

As to the possibility that you might starve, during those first days while you *are* hungry — the answer is simply that you *don't*. It is perfectly true that men have died of starvation in three or four days; but the starvation existed in their minds — it was fright that killed them. That they did not truly starve is proven by my letters from several hundreds of people who have fasted over that time, and who are alive to tell of it.

There are conditions in the human body which lead to death inevitably; and some of these conditions are beyond the power of the fast to remedy. When a person so afflicted sets out to fast, and dies in spite of the fast, the papers of course declare that he died because of the fast. Dr. L. B. Hazzard of Seattle has published a very useful little book, "Fasting for the Cure of Disease," in which she tells of two cases of "death from fasting," where the autopsy revealed conditions with which the fast had no connection, and which made death certain. Chances of that sort one has to take in life. You may have a blood vessel in such a state that when you run after a street car the increased pressure will cause it to burst; but you do not on that account declare that no man ought to exert himself violently.

As an example of the part that mental disturbances may play in the fast, I will cite the case of a woman friend who started out to fast for a complication of chronic ailments. She was rather stout, and did not mind it at all — was going cheerfully about her daily tasks; but her husband heard about it, and came home to tell her what a fool she was making of herself; and in a few hours she was in a state of complete collapse. No doubt if there had been a physician in the neighborhood, there would have been another tale of a "victim of a shallow and unscrupulous sensationalist." Fortunately, however, business called the husband away again, and the next day the woman was all right, and completed an eight-day fast with the best results. Bear this in mind, so that if you wake up some morning and find your temperature sub-normal and your pulse at forty, and your arms too weak to lift you, and if your friends get round you and tell you that you look like a mummy out of a sarcophagus of the seventeenth dynasty, and that I am a Socialist and an undesirable citizen — you may be able to smile at them good naturedly and tell them that you will never again eat until you are hungry.

I have thought over the cases of failure of the fast, where I have been able to inquire into all the circumstances, and I think I can make the statement that I do not know a case which might not be attributed either to the influence of nervous excitement, or to unwise breaking of the fast. In the last batch of letters was one with a printed account of the disastrous results of a three weeks' fast taken by a woman. It is an example of about all the blunders that I can think of. She describes herself as occupying "a responsible office position," which taxed her strength to the utmost; and she tried to do this work all the time she was fasting. She would get up and go to work when she was "scarcely able to drag one foot after another." On about the nineteenth day her mother arrived, and then I quote: "She almost dropped at sight of me, for I had not given a hint as to my condition; but despite my protests, she sent for the doctor at once. My! Did n't he scold, and tell me what was what! Mother's heart was so torn with sorrow and pity that she had n't the heart to reproach me for my three weeks' orgy of fasting. She thought I had paid dearly for my folly." I don't think it necessary to say anything more, except that I feel sorry for the victim, and that I am glad to know this happened two years ago, so that I am not to blame for the results.

By way of contrast with this case I will quote the following letter, which will show the reader the kind of experience that makes fasting enthusiasts: "My wife and I have each nearly reached our seventy-second year. I was born a physical wreck. A dozen years ago we began taking short fasts, from three to eleven days' duration, for all our ills of the flesh. But each of us had chronic troubles of forty years' standing, which seemed growing no better. And finally, two years ago last July, my wife said she was going to take a 'conquest fast' if it killed her, for she was tired of living with her present ills. I thought it a good time to try a little conquest fasting on my own hook. I had no fear of the result. I knew that nature would tell me when I had fasted long enough. So we began an absolute fast from all food except distilled water and fresh air. We lived in fresh air night and day. We took copious enemas daily, and I took a cabinet sweat, followed by a cold plunge every other day. I knew that I must have many years of filth accumulation in my bowels. And the amount of putridity that came from my bowels the first twenty-five days of the fast was amazing.

"After fasting twenty-eight days I began to be hungry, and broke my fast with a little grape juice, followed the next day with tomatoes, and later with vegetable soup. My wife began to be hungry after fasting thirty-one days, and broke her fast in a similar manner to myself.

"It is now two years since we took the conquest fast, and my wife has no return of her former troubles. And I am enjoying all the mental and physical pleasures which come from clean bowels. We think we have learned how to live that we will never need another fast. Soon after the fast I was examined by Dr. S——, the leading surgeon of Los Angeles and Southern California, who pronounced me as being the most wonderful person he ever met regarding softness of arteries, and suppleness of body, for my age."

## Fasting and the Mind

The reader will observe that I discuss this fasting question from a materialistic view-point. I am telling what it does to the body; but besides this, of course, fasting is a religious exercise. I heard the other day from a man who was taking a forty-day fast, as a means of increasing his "spiritual power." I am not saying that for you to smile at — he has excellent authority for the procedure. The point with me is that I find life so full of interest just now that I don't have much time to think about my "soul." I get so much pleasure out of a handful of raisins, or a cold bath, or a game of tennis, that I fear it is interfering with my spiritual development. I have, however, a very dear friend who goes in for the things of the soul, and she tells me that when you are fasting, the higher faculties are in a sensitive condition, and that you can do many interesting things with your subliminal self. For instance, she had always considered herself a glutton; and so, during an eight-day fast, just before going to sleep and just after awakening, she would lie in a sort of trance and impress upon her mind the idea of restraint in eating. The result, she declared, has been that she has never since then had an impulse to over-eat.

There are many such curious things, about which you may read in the books of the yogis and the theosophists — who were fasting in previous incarnations when you and I were swinging about in the tree-tops by our tails. But I ought to report upon one fasting experiment which resulted disastrously for me. Earlier in this book I told how I had been able to write the greater part of a play while fasting. Shortly afterwards I plunged into the writing of a new novel, and as usual I got so much interested in it that I was n't hungry. I said that I would fast, and save the eating time, and the digesting time as well. So I would sit and work for sixteen hours or more a day, sometimes for six hours at a stretch without moving. After two or three days of this I would be hungry, and would eat something; but being too much excited to digest it, I would say, "Hang eating, anyhow!" — and go on for another period of work. I kept that up for some six weeks, and I turned out an appalling lot of manuscript; but I found that I had taken off twenty-five pounds of flesh, and had got to such a point that I could not digest a little warm milk. I cite this in order that the reader may understand just why I take a gross and material view of fasting. My advice is to lie round in the sun and read story-books and take care of your body, and leave the soul-exercises and the nervous efforts until the fast is over. But all the same, I know that there will be great poetry written some day, when our poets have got on to the fasting trick — and when our poets care enough about their work to be willing to feed it with their own flesh.

The great thing about the fast is that it sets you

a new standard of health. You have been accustomed to worrying along somehow; but now you discover your own possibilities, and thereafter you are not content until you have found some way to keep that virginal state of stomach which one possesses for a month or two after a successful fast. It must mean, of course, many changes in your life, if you really wish to keep it. It means the giving up of tobacco and alcohol, and a too sedentary life, and steam-heated rooms; above all else, it means giving up self-indulgent eating.

A couple of years ago my wife and myself made the acquaintance of a young lady patient in a sanatorium, who was in a much run-down condition, anæmic and nervous. We persuaded her to take a fast of five or six days, and afterwards take the milk diet, as the result of which she went back to her home in Virginia with what she described as " smiles and dimples and curves and bright eyes." She was so enthusiastic about the cure that she proceeded to apply it to all her family and her friends; and some time afterwards she wrote my wife a most diverting account of her adventures. After some persuasion I secured her permission to quote her letter, having duly omitted all the names. It makes clear the thorny path which the fasting enthusiast has to travel in this world.

I will try in a very limited space of time to tell you what keeps me a slave here at home. I got Mr. X—— down from —— to put papa and mamma on the fasting cure — papa had a bad case of grippe — mamma had indigestion. My oldest married brother is in dreadful health, and his wife and baby are not well. I wore myself nearly out trying to get them well, and at the same time trying to pick up some threads of long neglected social duties. People were beginning to call me "stuck-up" (horrid vulgar term), so unless I wanted to make enemies of the wives and daughters of papa's and brother's business friends, I had to go to a few parties and pay some long-neglected calls. I did it all, and then decided to have Mr. X—— come to help me. I got papa and mamma and M—— and *her baby* (!) on a fast — and then woe is me — I had to get them off again! They had various and alarming symptoms due to their ignorance of the methods, and the wild interest of the town medicine-men. The family doctor gave me a "straight talk" and asked me if I was going to try *to kill my father and mother.* Papa would not give up his cigarettes, and a "toddy" now and then. M——'s baby lost four pounds while his mother was fasting. All the doctors' wives came to call, and beset me with questions — and I had the d—— of a time. But I stood by my guns. When the overfed, self-indulgent family all got to vomiting at once, my hands were full, and I nearly had nervous prostration before I got order out of the bedlam I had stirred up.

Well, they got over the fast and on to the milk. Then I had to tend to the milk myself or they refused to drink it. Finally mamma got to feeling so well that she sat up, and planned big course dinners and invited people to eat them. She began to order new clothes for the kids, new furnishings for the house, and started in to live her disorderly, ungodly "Southern hospitality" life all over again. Our senator died and mamma got into politics in the new election; and Cousin J—— got drunk, and I had to go with him to the Keeley Institute, etc., etc. Surely there is a heaven for saints like me. I did not fly the roost as I was tempted to do, but I answered midnight calls of the spoiled, nauseated ones, and fixed hot-water bags, quelled riots among the meat-eating servants and hungry children — and swore I'd win! I did. Well, I got things going in fine order at last, with papa cured of his grippe and an old case of kidney trouble. Mamma is now comfortably eating boiled ham and stuffed peppers, and fruit cake and cherry pie, and green olives and what not at the same meal. She is well, though. But of course she will get sick again. Papa, the only sane member of our family, is still holding on to the milk, taking four quarts of buttermilk a day, and he is flourishing, thank heaven! M—— is still bilious, having broken her fast with hard-boiled eggs and pork chops. And I am still living, in spite of having been to Keeley, and incidentally having danced all night (with a low-neck, short-sleeved gown on!) at the —— Club ball, sat through several dinners and bridge parties into the "wee sma' hours," and had two men propose to me with the prelude, "You are the nicest, most refined, and most lovable girl in the world if you *are* a crank." Was n't that a nice beginning for a proposal of marriage? I accepted them both on condition that I be allowed to remain a crank.

Well, the next chapter began with an old lover who had married another woman. He came to see me and said he had a tape-worm! Ye gods — such romance! His wife had stomach and intestinal trouble. I turned Mr. X—— over to them, and them over to Mr. X——. The lady got along, but the poor man with a wild beast inside him got so sick after an eight-day fast that he wanted to have me mobbed, sent for two trained nurses and four doctors — this is no exaggeration — the doctors looked at me, and looks were as plain as words — "You little devil! You did it for pure meanness." For three days my poor friend had the doctors giving him hypodermics, and he never stopped vomiting until we were all nearly dead. Then he quieted down, got well, ate a beef-steak with a few dozen oysters and mushrooms, and took me riding in his new automobile. The grim humor in the whole thing is that if I had not gotten my roses and dimples and curves and bright eyes back by fasting, this man would never have taken me riding in his new automobile. Take a tip from me — all the good nursing and friendly efforts in behalf of the health of my friends did not endear me to them one half as much as the plump, rosy smile I wore with my new silk gown. The first day our sick friend went out in his car — alas for the ways of human nature — masculine human nature, I mean — I told him so. And he agreed with me and ended by saying, "Darn an ugly woman — I 'll forgive a pretty one *anything*."

## Diet after the Fast

Many people write me, begging me to outline for them the ideal diet. I used to do that sort of thing, but I have stopped; having come to realize that we are still at the beginning of our diet-experiments. I have done a good deal of experimenting myself, and have made some interesting discoveries. I have lived for a week on fruit only, and again on wheat only; I have lived for three weeks on nothing but milk, and again on nothing but beef-steak. I have lived for a year on raw food, and for over three years I professed the religion of vegetarianism. For the last two months I have lived on beef-steak, shredded wheat, raisins and fresh fruit; but by the time this book appears I may be trying sour milk and dates — somebody told me about that the other day, and it sounds good to me. Some of my correspondents object to my willingness to try new diets; they write me that they find it bewildering, and think it indicative of an unstable mind. They do not realize that I am exacting in my demands — I want a diet which will permit me to overwork with impunity. I have n't found it yet, but I am on the way; and meantime I make my experiments with a light heart, for I always know that if anything goes wrong, I can take a fast and start afresh.

The general rules are mostly of a negative sort. There are many kinds of foods, some of them most generally favored, of which one may say that they should never be used, and that those who use them can never be as well as they would be without them. Such foods are all that contain alcohol or vinegar; all that contain cane sugar; all that contain white flour in any one of its thousand alluring forms of bread, crackers, pie, cake, and puddings; and all foods that have been fried — by which I mean cooked with grease, whether that grease be lard, or butter, or eggs or milk. It is my conviction that one should bar these things at the outset, and admit of no exceptions. I do not mean to say that healthy men and women cannot eat such things and be well; but I say that they cannot be as well as they would be without them; and that every particle of such food they eat renders them more liable to all sorts of infection, and sows in their systems the seeds of the particular chronic disease that is to lay them low sooner or later.

There are a number of other things, which I do not rate as quite so bad, but which we bar in our family — simply because they are not so good. For instance, I am inclined to regard beans as being too difficult of digestion and too liable to fermentation to be eaten by any one who can get anything better. And I personally do not eat peanuts, because I have found that I do not digest them; and I do not use milk (except in the exclusive milk diet), because it is constipating, and I have a tendency in that direction. Almost everyone will discover idiosyncrasies of that sort in his own system. One person cannot digest cheese, another cannot digest bananas, another cannot stand the taste of olive oil. You may read a glowing account of some diet system by which some other person has worked miracles, and you may try it, and persist in it for a long time, and finally come to realize that it was the worst diet you could possibly have been following. I have always counted orange juice as the ideal food with which to break a fast; yet a friend whom I was advising broke his fast with the juice of half an orange, and had a violent cramp. He had been so confiding in my greater knowledge that he had omitted to tell me that any sort of acid fruit had always made him ill.

Such things as this are of course not natural;

but a perfectly normal and well person is, under the artificial conditions of our bringing up, a very great rarity; and so we all have to regard ourselves as more or less diseased, and work towards the ideal of soundness. We must do this with intelligence — there is no short cut, no way to save one's self the trouble of thinking.

I used to think there was. I would discover this or that wonderful new diet-wrinkle, and I would go round preaching it to all my friends, and making a general nuisance of myself. And some one would try it, and it would not work; and often, to my own humiliation, I would discover that it was not working in my own case half so well as I had thought it was.

By way of setting an ideal, let me give you the example of a young lady who for six or seven months has been living in our home, and giving us a chance to observe her dietetic habits. This young lady three years ago was an anæmic school-teacher, threatened with consumption, and a victim of continual colds and headaches; miserable and beaten, with an exopthalmic goitre which was slowly choking her to death. She fasted eight days, and achieved a perfect cure. She is to-day bright, alert and athletic; and she lives on about twelve hundred calories of food a day — one half what I eat, and less than a third of the old-school dietetic standards. Occasionally she will eat nut butter, or sweet potato, or some whole wheat crackers with butter, or a dish of ice-cream; but at least ninety per cent of her food has consisted of fresh fruit. Meal after meal, day after day, I have seen her eat one or two bananas and two or three peaches, or say, a slice of watermelon or canteloupe; at some meals she will eat only the peaches, and then again she will eat nothing. A dollar a week would pay for all her food; and on this diet she laughs and talks, reads and thinks, walks and swims with my wife and myself — a kind of external dietetic conscience, which we would find it hard to get along without. And tell me, Dr. Woods Hutchinson, or other scoffer at the "food-faddists," don't you think that a case like this gives us some right to ask for patient investigation of our claims? Or will you stand by your pill boxes and your carving-knives and the rest of your paraphernalia, and compel us to cure all your patients in spite of you?

# THE USE OF MEAT

I AM asked many questions as to my attitude toward the question of meat-eating. I was brought up on a diet of meat, bread and butter, potatoes, and sweet things. Four years ago when I found myself desperately run down, suffering from nervousness, insomnia, and almost incessant headaches, I came upon various articles written by vegetarians, and I began to suspect that my trouble might be due to meat. I went away on a camping-trip for several weeks, taking no meat with me, and because I found that I was a great deal better, I believed that the meat had been responsible for my trouble. I then visited the Battle Creek Sanitarium, and became familiar with all their arguments against meat, and thereafter I did not use it for three years. I called myself a vegetarian; but at the same time I realized that I differed from most vegetarians in some important particulars.

For instance, I had never taken any stock in the arguments for vegetarianism upon the moral side. It has always seemed to me that human beings have a right to eat meat, if meat is necessary for their best development, either physical or mental. I have never had any sympathy with that "humanitarianism" which tells us that it is our duty to regard pigs and chickens as our brothers. I was listening the other day to one of these enthusiasts, who had been reading aloud one of the "Uncle Remus" stories, and who went on in touching language to set forth the fact that his vegetable garden constituted one place where "Bre'r Rabbit" was free to wander at will and to help himself; and he described how happy it made him to see these gentle animals hopping about among his cabbages, having lost all their fear of him. That sort of thing will work very well so long as it is confined to one farm, and so long as there is a hunting season upon all the other farms in the locality; but let the humanitarians proceed to apply their regimen in a whole state, and they will soon have so many billions of rabbits hopping about among their cabbages that they will have to choose between shooting rabbits or having no cabbages.

The reader, I presume, is familiar with calculations which show the rate at which rabbits multiply, how many tens and hundreds of millions would be produced by a single pair of rabbits in ten years. It should be quite obvious that the time would come when all human beings would be spending their energies in planting gardens to support rabbits; and that if ever they stopped planting gardens, there would be a famine for the rabbits, with infinitely more suffering than is involved in the present method of keeping them down. Also, even though the humanitarians might have their way with men, the hawks and the owls and the foxes would probably remain unregenerate. I remember, when I was a small boy, being sternly rebuked by an agitated maiden lady who discovered me throwing stones at a squirrel. Not so many days afterwards, however, the lady discovered the squirrel engaged in carrying off young birds from a nest outside her window, and she found her theories about "kindness to dumb animals" rudely disturbed.

The same thing, it seems to me, is still more true of domestic animals. Domestic animals survive on earth solely because of the protection of man, and for the sake of the benefits they bring to him. If it is necessary to human health and well-being to slaughter a cow rather than to wait and let her die of old age and lingering disease, it seems to me that nothing but mawkish sentimentality would protest.

It is pointed out to us what places of cruelty and filth our slaughter-houses are; the reader may believe that I learned something about this in my preparations for the writing of "The Jungle." But then this is not necessarily true about slaughter-houses — any more than it is necessarily true that railroads must kill and maim a couple of hundred thousand people in this country every year. In Europe they have municipal slaughter-houses which are constructed upon scientific lines, and in which no filth is permitted to accumulate; also they have devised means for the killing of animals which are painless. In the stockyards I have seen a man standing upon a gallery, leaning over and pounding at the head of a steer with a hammer, and making half a dozen blows before he succeeded in knocking down the terrified animal. In Europe, on the other hand, they fit over the head of the animal a leathern cap, which has in it a steel spike; a single tap upon the head of this spike is sufficient to drive it into the animal's brain, causing instant insensibility.

And it must be borne in mind also that the sufferings of dumb animals are entirely different from our own. They do not suffer the pains of anticipation. A cow walks into a slaughter-house without fear, and stands still and permits a leathern cap to be fitted over its head without suspicion; and while it is placidly grazing in the field, it is untroubled by any consciousness of the fact that next week it will be hanging in a butcher's shop as beef. I recall in this connection an observation of that wise philosopher, Mr. Dooley, concerning the inhumanities of vegetarianism. He said that it had always seemed to him a very cruel thing "to cut off a young tomato in its prime, or to murder a whole cradle full of baby peas in the pod."

These things will convince the devotee of the religion of vegetarianism that I am a lost soul, and always have been. Perhaps so. I try to guide my conduct by scientific knowledge; what I ask to know about the question of meat-eating is the actual facts of its effect upon the human organism — the amount of energy which it develops, the diseases which it causes, or, on the contrary, the immunity to disease which it claims to confer; also, of course, its cheapness and convenience as an article of diet. Some evidence of this sort we possess; but very little, it seems to me, in proportion to the importance of the subject. Professor Fisher has conducted some thorough experiments as to the influence of meat-eating upon endurance, which seem to develop the fact that vegetarians possess a far greater amount of endurance than meat-eaters. These experiments are what we want, but they seemed to me, when I read them, to be weak in one or two important particulars. They did not tell us what the vegetarians ate, nor what the meat-eaters ate. Those who are vegetarians at the present day are very apt to be people who have given some thought to the question of diet, and have attempted to adopt sounder ways of life; while, on the other hand, meat-eaters are generally people who have given no thought to the question of health at all — they are very apt to be smokers and drinkers as well as meat-eaters. Also it is to be pointed out that endurance is not the only factor of importance to our physical well-being.

There have been numerous expositions of the greater liability of meat to contamination. Dr. Kellogg, for instance, has purchased specimens of meat in the butcher-shops, and has had them examined under the microscope, and has told us how many hundreds of millions of bacteria to the gram have been discovered. This argument has a tendency to appal one; I know it had great effect upon me for a long time, and I took elaborate pains to take into my system only those kinds of food which were sterilized, or practically so. This is the health regimen which is advocated by Professor Metchnikoff; one should eat only foods which have been thoroughly boiled and sterilized. I have come, in the course of time, to the conclusion that this way of living is suicidal, and that there is no way of destroying one's health more quickly. I think that the important question is, not how many bacteria there are in the food when you swallow it, but how many bacteria there come to be in food after it gets into your alimentary canal. The digestive juices are apparently able to take care of a very great number of germs; it is after the food has passed on down, and is lodged in the large intestine, that the real fermentation and putrefaction begin — and these count for more, in the question of health, than that which goes on in the butcher-shop or the refrigerator or the pantry.

Do not misunderstand what I mean by this. I am not advocating that anyone should swallow the bacteria of deadly diseases, such as typhoid and cholera; I am not advocating that anyone should use food which is in a state of decomposition — on the contrary, I have ruled out of my dietary a number of foods in common use which depend for their production upon bacterial action; for instance, beer and wine, and all alcoholic drinks, all kinds of cheeses, sauerkraut, vinegar, etc. My point is simply that the ordinary healthy person has no reason for terrifying himself about the common aërobic bacteria — which swarm in the atmosphere, and are found by hundreds of millions in all raw food, and in cooked food which has not been kept with the elaborate precautions that a surgeon uses with his instruments and linen; also that the real problem is to take into the system those foods which can be readily digested and assimilated, and which afford the body all the elements that it needs to keep itself in the best condition for the inevitable, incessant warfare with the hostile organisms which surround it.

So far as meat is concerned, of course no sensible person would use meat which showed the slightest trace of being spoiled, nor any meat which had been canned, or ground up and made into messes, such as sausage. If one uses reasonably fresh meat, the bacteria which may be on the outside of it will be killed by proper cooking. And so the question is, it seems to me, what does meat do after it gets into the stomach? And that is a matter for practical experiment, which very few people have made, so far as I have any information. Innumerable people are eating meat, of course; but they are eating it in combination with all other kinds of destructive foods, and they are eating it prepared in innumerable unwholesome ways. So far as I know, no scientist has ever taken a group of normal men and kept them for a certain period upon a rational vegetarian diet, and then put them for another period upon a diet containing broiled fresh meat, and made a thoroughly scientific study of their condition, as, for instance, Professor Chittenden did for his "low proteid" experiments.

For about a year previous to reading about Dr. Salisbury's "meat diet," I had been following the raw-food regimen. I had gained wonderful results from this, and I had written a good deal about it; but I had got these results while leading an active life, and not doing hard brain-work. I found continually that when I settled down to a sedentary life, and to writing which involved a great nervous strain, I began to lose weight on raw food; and if I kept on with this regimen, I would begin to have headaches, and other signs of distress from what I was eating. As an illustration of what I mean, I might say that quite recently I plunged into a novel in which I was very much absorbed, and I lost twelve pounds in sixteen days; and this, it must be understood, without changing my diet in the slightest particular. I went on with the work for about six weeks, and by that time I had lost twenty pounds. In explaining this to myself, I was divided between uncertainty as to whether I was working too hard, or whether I was eating too much. Finally I took the precaution to weigh what I was eating, and to make quite certain that

I was eating no more than I had been accustomed to eat during periods when I had remained at my normal weight. I then cut the quantity of my food in half, and found that I lost much less rapidly. This served to convince me that the trouble lay in the fact that I had not sufficient nervous energy left to assimilate the food that I was taking.

And I have known others to have this same experience. Bernarr Macfadden, in particular, told me that he could not get along upon the nut and fruit diet while closely confined in his office, and that he found the solution of his problem in milk. Inasmuch as there is nothing that poisons me quite so quickly as milk, I had to look farther for my solution. As a matter of fact, I had been looking for this solution for more than ten years, though it is only quite recently that I had come to understand the problem clearly. It is a problem which every brain-worker faces; and I am sure, therefore, that there will be many who will find the report of my experiments and blunders to be of interest to them. I have tried, under these circumstances, all kinds of the more digestible foods — toast, rice, baked potatoes, baked apples, milk, poached eggs, and so on; always I have found that these foods digested perfectly, but they poisoned my system because of their constipating effect; and this was a dilemma which I was never able to get around.

I now read Dr. Salisbury's book, "The Relation of Alimentation to Disease." Many of his experiments I found extremely interesting. Dr. Salisbury described the consequences of the ordinary starch and sugar diet as making a "yeast-pot" of one's intestinal tract. I found in my own case many of the symptoms which he described, and I determined to see what would be the effect of the meat diet in my case.

I began the experiment with reluctance. I had lost all interest in the taste of meat, and I had a prejudice against it; I hated the smell of it, and I hated the feeling of it, and I was prepared for the direst consequences, according to the prophecies of my vegetarian friends. I should not have been at all surprised if I had been made very ill by my first meal. I was prepared to allow for that, supposing that after three years I had perhaps forgotten how to digest meat. To my surprise, however, I found no difficulty at all. I soon gave up preparing the meat according to the elaborate prescription of Dr. Salisbury, and contented myself simply with eating good lean beef-steak. I continued the experiment for two weeks, living upon meat exclusively. I found that all my symptoms of stomach trouble disappeared, and I had no headaches whatever. I got quite weak upon the exclusive diet, but this was according to Dr. Salisbury's statement; just as soon as I added a little shredded wheat biscuit and dried fruit to the menu this trouble disappeared, and I gained in weight with great rapidity, and was soon back where I had been before.

I did not continue the diet, owing partly to distaste for it, and partly to the inconvenience of it. I had accustomed myself to the raw food way of living, and any one who knows what this means can understand my distaste for washing plates and scraping frying-pans, and going to the bother of getting fresh meat and keeping it and cooking it. Also, of course, there was the item of expense. Upon the raw-food diet I had been able to live for ten cents a day. I am never accustomed to spending more than thirty or forty cents a day, even when indulging in abundant fresh fruit.

Perhaps I ought also to specify that a good deal of the success of the diet may have been owing to the hot-water regimen which is a part of it. An hour or two before every meal one is supposed to sip at least a pint of very hot water, which has the effect of cleansing out the stomach, and stimulates peristaltic action to a remarkable degree. I had been accustomed to drink hot water while fasting, but I had never taken it systematically, as I did at this time. It is a trick well worth knowing about.

I ought also to mention the fact that I suggested to several others that they try this meat diet. One of them, a friend who had been eating raw food at my suggestion, with the very best results, began the experiment and continued for three days, and the results were most disappointing. This friend, a woman in middle years, became very ill, with all the symptoms of stomach trouble, diarrhoea, and general poisoning. She wrote me that she gave up the diet at the end of three days, because she saw no use in making herself desperately ill. She added: "I followed the regimen in every smallest detail, precisely according to Dr. Salisbury's direction. You know me, and you know that when I do a thing I do it thoroughly, so there is no need to say any more about that." Which only goes to show that, as the proverb has it, "One man's meat is another man's poison."

Dr. Salisbury recommends the meat diet especially in cases of tuberculosis. He finds that the predisposing cause of this disease is "vegetable fermentation." He declares that the excessive starch and sugar diet leads to the production of yeast spores and other ferments in the intestinal tract, and that these are absorbed into the circulation and ultimately clog the small capillaries in the lungs. Dr. Salisbury's theory was set forth over thirty years ago, and that was before Koch had made his discovery of the tubercle bacillus. This discovery would seem to put Dr. Salisbury's theory out of court altogether; but as we physical culturists are inclined to suspect, there are causes of disease lying behind the attack of the specific bacillus. These causes are a depleted blood supply and a weakened system; and it seems to me, from what I have observed of consumptives and their diet, that Dr. Salisbury's theories fit in very well indeed with the Koch theory.

I wrote recently to Professor Chittenden to ask him what, in his opinion, would be the effects of the meat diet upon tuberculosis. He replied that he knew no reason for believing that it would be of special benefit but that the whole subject of diet in tuberculosis seemed to him to be one concerning which there was urgent need of experiment and investigation. This is unquestionably the case. I know no two physicians who seem to agree in the diets they prescribe to consumptives, and I have never met two consumptives who followed the same regimen. The general idea seems to be to stuff as much food in your system as you possibly can, especially milk and raw eggs; and it seems to me quite certain that, whatever system may be correct, this system is incorrect.

This much seems to me to be clear: tuberculosis is a disease brought about by under-nourishment. It is a disease to which the poor are especially liable; and while this is undoubtedly in part due to bad air, it is also due to bad feeding. And when ignorant people wish to live cheaply, the foods they eat are the sugar and starch foods. I remember in Thoreau's "Walden" he sets forth how he lived for many months upon five or six dollars' worth of food. He does not give the amount of the food by weight, so of course we cannot tell exactly; but he gives the prices he paid, and the leading articles in his diet were flour, rice, corn-meal, molasses, sugar and lard. One is, therefore, perfectly prepared to learn that Thoreau died of consumption. And the same thing, I believe, will happen to a good many enthusiastic vegetarians of my acquaintance. They have given up meat, and they have made up for it by increasing their consumption of bread and crackers, rice and potatoes, and prepared and pre-digested cereals, which they eat with cream and sugar. Even when they use high proteid food, it is in some form such as beans, which contain a great deal of starch, and in a form which is difficult of digestion. As a result of this, they are thin and anæmic looking — they do not seem to be able to put on flesh by means of intellectual fervor and an optimistic philosophy. The result of my meat-diet experiment has been to convince me yet more firmly that the cooked-vegetable diet is the worst diet in the world for myself. (I am content to phrase it that way, and leave it for others to find out about their own case.) There has been some agitation in vegetarian circles since the report has gone around that I have become a backslider, and have gone back to the flesh-pots. I state the facts here for what they may be worth to others. I shall never call myself a "vegetarian" again — though I shall be a vegetarian the greater part of the time.

For it should be noted, of course, that the objections which I have brought against the cooked vegetarian diet do not apply at all to the raw-food diet, which is entirely a different matter. If one lives upon nuts, whole grains boiled or shredded, salad vegetables and fruits, he does not get an excess of either starch or sugar, but a perfectly balanced dietary, every article of which is rich in natural salts — in which the starchy foods, and especially the prepared cereals, are fatally deficient. Such a diet can be followed by any person in normal health, who is leading a physically active life. I have known a number of people, old and young, to start out upon this way of life without any preliminaries, and they have noted a great gain in health and efficiency, and have had no trouble of any sort. This diet is as cheap as the bean and white flour and rice diet of the ordinary "vegetarian," and it is, by all odds, the simplest and most convenient diet in the world.

I have been accustomed all my life to think of meat as a very "heavy" article of food, an article of food suited for men doing hard physical labor; it is a curious fact that the view I am setting forth here is precisely the opposite. So long as I am doing hard physical labor, whether it is walking ten miles a day, or playing tennis, or building a house, I get along perfectly upon the raw food; but when I settle down for long periods of thinking and writing — often sitting for six hours without moving from one position — I find that I need something else, and nothing has answered that purpose quite so well as beef-steak. It appears to be, so far as I am concerned, the most easily digested and most easily assimilated of foods. And because the work that I am doing seems to me to be important, I am willing to make the sacrifice of money and time and trouble which it necessitates. My diet at such times will consist of beef or chicken, shredded wheat biscuit, and a little fruit. If any one is disposed to follow my example and make this experiment, I beg to call his attention especially to the fact that I name these three kinds of food, and none others; and that I mean these three kinds and none others. The main trouble with advising anybody to eat meat is that he proceeds to eat it in the every-day world, where it means not the eating of broiled lean beef, but also of bacon and eggs, and of bread and butter, and of potatoes with cream gravy, and of rice pudding and crackers and cheese and coffee. Please do not proceed to eat these things and then hold meat-eating responsible for the consequences.

I do not for a moment wish to give the impression that I believe that meat-eating is necessary to a normally active person, or that humanity will always continue to eat meat. No invention of science can ever make meat as cheap a food as nuts and fruit, and nothing can ever make it as beautiful or attractive a food, nor as clean a food, nor as easily prepared a food. I believe that children can be brought up without knowing the taste of meat, and can be trained to lead normal and active lives from the very beginning, and can live on the raw-food diet and thrive. What I am discussing here are my own experiences, and I do not regard myself as a normal specimen of humanity, because I work a great deal harder than anybody has a right to work. I do that because there are so many idle and useless people in the world at present — and some have to make martyrs of themselves, until conditions of injustice and cruelty have been done away with.

# APPENDIX

## Some Letters from Fasters

London, Ontario, May 2, 1910.

Dear Sir, — Your article in a recent magazine very greatly interested me. My sister, on her way home from a five-and-a-half-weeks' visit in Boston and New York, where she had been endeavoring to discover the causes of her frightful headaches, bought that number of the magazine and read your experience, with, as you can well imagine, a deep interest. In Boston she had consulted one of the two physicians supposed to head the profession (as consultants) in that city. This man told her she had Bright's disease and leakage of the heart, and he gave her ten years to live — if she was very careful. As she has five children under twelve years of age, this was a sad outlook. She weighed 122 pounds when she left — and this was the lowest weight since early girlhood — but on her return, weighed on the same scales in the same clothing, she was only 108 pounds. She looked *very* bad, and her spirits were at zero.

Your article appealed to her, and she would have unhesitatingly tried your remedy, but that she was pregnant, and thought it would probably mean the child's death. The Boston obstetrician, who was consulted, said, if the other doctor's diagnosis was correct, the child would have to be taken at eight months.

After reading your experience, I said to my sister: "You cannot perhaps follow Mr. Sinclair's example, but you can approximate to it. If you go to your own doctor he will undoubtedly send you to some sanatorium where the patients are fairly stuffed. Suppose you come over to my place each noon and take dinner, having eaten only *a very light breakfast;* then rest from two to five, take a long bath when you rise, go for a walk from six to six-thirty, and then to your own home for tea, taking only a shredded wheat biscuit for that meal."

My sister consented, and on Saturday was weighed. On that light diet, and in twelve days, she had gained fourteen pounds. Her color is returning, she does not tire as she did, and we are full of hope that she may recover.

My object in writing was to thank you for your frank recital of ills and aches and their cure, and to get from you the names of the books to which you referred.

Several of my friends have read your articles on my recommendation, and one at least is seriously considering a lengthened fast. Reading the article took me back to the "no-breakfast régime," which I followed for five years, and then, for no especial reason, abandoned. Already I feel much better.

Sincerely and gratefully,

M. R. T.

SKOWHEGAN, MAINE, May 30, 1910.

DEAR SIR, — I read your article in the *Cosmopolitan* with deep interest, and am to-day on my seventh day's fast. My sensations thus far are exactly like yours. I shall fast until hunger returns, if it take a month.

My age is forty-eight, and I have enjoyed the best of health nearly all my life. Even now my digestion is all right, but for five years or so I have been troubled with rheumatism, not the painful, swelling sort, but lame joints.

I tried "Fletcherism," and for the last nine months have done my best to live up to his suggestions, but fell down, exactly as in your own case. I can't tell what to eat, or when I have eaten enough.

Whether this fast of yours does me any permanent good or not, my joints certainly move better to-day than for six months, and I have every confidence in the theory. The physicians here to a man all laugh at me, likewise my friends. I had lost ten pounds in weight at the end of the sixth day; I lost three the first, two each for the next two days, and a pound a day for the next three days.

You speak of an unmistakable appetite. I could eat, of course, now, though I have no appetite, and I am wondering how I shall know when a real appetite returns. Mrs. W. is as keen to try the fasting cure as I, and her condition is very like Mrs. Sinclair's, but I thought one member of the family was enough for the first try-out. Please pardon a total stranger for encroaching upon the time of a busy man, but in the hunt for health, without which life is not worth living, one will do things he would not otherwise think of. For your information I will say that I have attended to my office and business every day since my fast began, walking to my home and back at least three times daily, for the exercise; driving a touring-car nights and Sunday, for pleasure, exactly as though there had been no change in my habits. The strangest part of the experience is that I feel so well, and except for a slight faintness, feel perfectly well to-day. Say — but I was hungry for the first two days!

Yours truly,
HERBERT WENTWORTH.

CLYDE PARK, MONT., May 17, 1910.

DEAR SIR, — I was much interested in your article in the *Cosmopolitan* on "Starving for Health's Sake." For some time before I read it I had been troubled with a coated tongue and a nasty, bitter taste in my mouth. When I read the article my complaint was probably at its worst. I consulted a doctor, who gave me some capsules to clean out my intestinal canal, so he said. I asked him what I could eat and he said, "The less you eat the better." So I ate nothing for a week. Everything connected with my fast for that week was just as you described it — a ravenous hunger on the second day and after that no hunger at all. However, the coated tongue was still there, and when I next saw the doctor I mentioned your article and said you recommended rectal injections.

He said he read your article and approved of it, and said after a thorough examination that I had an impaction of the colon. He said he would give me something to work on my colon and also added that if I fasted long enough the impaction would move out of itself. He also recommended injections. On the 25th day, although the coated tongue and nasty taste were still with me, I commenced eating again, as there was so much work to do on the ranch, and I had to do it, as hired help was scarce. I drank nothing but tepid water and very thin lemonade, slightly sweetened, during my fast of twenty-four days. I dropped from 175 pounds to 143 pounds.

It is a week now since I broke my fast and I am rapidly gaining weight. Yesterday I weighed 152 pounds. However, as I said, I still have the coated tongue, although not so bad as formerly, and when I regain more weight, I 'm going to begin another fast. I am fifty-three years of age, and have never used tea, coffee, whisky, or tobacco. I want to read up on the subject, so that when I begin again I 'll know what to do. Your article was all the literature I had on the subject, and it may have been incomplete in a great many important particulars.

Respectfully yours,

ROBERT AITKIN.

CHICAGO, ILL., May 22, 1910.

DEAR SIR, — I think you will be interested to learn the experience of my wife, who tried your fast, with the same results as your wife, over which we are very much delighted.

Allow me to say that it was all done on the quiet, and no one knew of it until it was all over. And then, of course, every one thought she was raving crazy, but she has since shown her friends that it was just the thing to do.

In the first place it appealed to her, and she went into it with *faith.* She fasted for eleven days, after the second day was never hungry at all, and really began to take nourishment before she was hungry.

The whole thing came out exactly as in your cases and was most interesting. She had temperature the first two days and ate crushed ice. After that, hot or cold water as desired. The tongue was coated very badly and her breath very bad. The tongue cleared very slowly and was quite discouraging, but after a few days was clear again. She lost over ten pounds, all of which has been regained and more, too, and she is gaining all the time. Complexion very clear, and the picture of health. Appetite great, eats everything, no aches or pains of any kind, and, best of all, no constipation, which was what she tried the fast for. She lost no strength to speak of and did n't have to take to bed at all; in fact, did everything about the house as usual.

Everything has been fine now for three weeks, and if the troubles return, she is to fast again and do it right, and will take no nourishment until the tongue clears.

She took internal baths nearly every day, and

was astonished at the results when nothing but water was being taken. While we don't recommend it for every one, it certainly has been a godsend in this case, and I believe because it was done right and with faith that it was just the thing for her. You certainly have one convert, and if this interests you, shall be pleased to know it.

Yours very sincerely,

C. D. F.

KNOXVILLE, TENN., June 5, 1910.

DEAR SIR, — I wish to acknowledge my indebtedness to you for a restoration to such health of body and clarity of mind as I have not known since my sixteenth year, when first I entered the high school. That was twenty years ago.

I read your article, "Starving for Health's Sake," in the *Cosmopolitan*, and, as you may recollect, asked you for information as to certain books treating of the fast as a cure for disease.

Instead of answering me fully, you referred my case to the Bernarr Macfadden Institution in Chicago, for which I thank you, but I did not go there because I had neither time nor money for that purpose.

Through a local book-dealer I ordered a copy of "Fasting, Hydrotherapy and Exercise," but after two weeks of waiting it failed to arrive, so with your *Cosmopolitan* article as my only guide and sum total of knowledge as to the fast, I quit eating on May 13 and did not take anything except water until the morning of May 26. Even then I was not hungry, but as I did not care to remain away from work any longer I broke the fast on the morning of the 26th. I lost thirteen pounds in weight, but was never too weak not to move around. I worked in the office for seven days, and the balance of the time remained at home, basking in the sunshine and reading constantly.

My health and appetite are in such perfect condition I can eat anything without fear of ulterior consequences.

As a result of the fast, I have sloughed off all my impedimenta of disease. Constipation of ten years' standing is gone as if by magic. Piles and resulting pruritis of eight years' tearing torture are nightmares of the past. Bronchitis and eczema of scalp have vanished. Asthma, due to nervous sympathy with the pneumogastric nerve, is no more. Catarrhal deafness, sore throat, intestinal catarrh, and a general neurasthenic condition have left me. Work was never so pleasant. I cannot get enough of physical exercise, it seems; my muscles seem to grow stronger as the exercise proceeds, and my weight is going upward about a pound daily. I am now three pounds heavier than I was before my fast began.

Life was never so beautiful, hope and joy never so green, the future for me and humanity's great movement toward a better day and higher good of existence never seemed so reasonable and possible of every realization as now, in the full possession of physical health and mental strength which have come back to me.

Heretofore my work has been wrought out in pain.

I am through with drugs. I graduated from allopathy long ago, then took up homeopathy and have now discarded it. I have spent over $500 in the last ten years trying to get well on medicines. These professional quacks bled me for a living and knew not how to cure me. Your article was written in the spirit of wishing to help suffering man. It cost me only thirty cents to use your method, viz.: six feet of rubber tubing to make a siphon to take two enemas daily. For that thirty cents I obtained relief a million-fold more beneficial than from $500 worth of medicine. Nay more, from your fasting idea I got rid of $500 worth of poisoning during ten years of medical superstition.

Sincerely yours,

H. E. HOOVER.

NORTHWEST SOCIETY ARCHAEOLOGICAL INSTITUTE OF AMERICA

WASHINGTON UNIVERSITY, SEATTLE, WASH.

Nov. 5, 1910.

EDITOR *Cosmopolitan* MAGAZINE.

Am enclosing clipping which shows that prominent men up here in the great Northwest are not afraid to try out certain methods of fighting disease merely because they are thought to be "new" or "faddy" (tho' in truth the fast cure is as old as the Old Testament).

The value of Professor Colvin's fast experience seems to be that he has given to the world the best method of breaking the fast and getting on to a solid-food diet. Upton Sinclair said the breaking of the fast is the most important part of it, and would be the most dangerous were it not for the great natural food, milk, which tides you over. But he fails to remember there are thousands with whom milk does not agree, sick or well.

Shortly after interview noted in enclosed clipping from Seattle *Times*, Professor Colvin attempted to begin to break the fast with orange juices and utterly failed. He then tried milk and was made so sick that he had to fast for three more days to get into a condition to break the fast. He then started in with a very light veal broth (not soup, nor tea). He soon got so he could take a cup of it every hour and a half. To get on to solid food he tried a few crackers with the broth, but found too much soda in the crackers and abandoned their use. Finally he hit upon the very thing that fitted the condition of his body, dry whole-wheat bread toasted. This toasted whole-wheat bread he had his cook crush with a rolling pin into a powder and each day mixed more of it with the cup of broth. After this he filled the cup three-fourths full of this toast powder and only poured in as much broth as the dust would absorb, making a solid gruel, which was very appetizing and nourishing (so much so that the professor continues to use it for breakfast food though his fast is closed). Now to this gruel he added mashed baked potato from time to time (more each time) until he virtually supplanted the toast dust. From this he went to baked apple, thence to raw eggs, thence to macaroni, thence to pigeon squab, and thence to solid earth.

It seems to me that his discovery of the broth-toast-gruel method is a great discovery. Especially so for those who live in the cities and cannot be sure as to the absolute purity of their milk. Even when the milk diet can be used it does not afford a solution for getting off of a liquid diet on to a solid food basis.

In your July number appears a letter from Mr. Buel of New York in which he says that it would be almost criminal to permit any one advanced in years to enter upon the dangerous folly of the "fast cure." I am enclosing you a clipping from the *Oregonian*, telling of the fasting experiences of Professor Colvin's friend, Rev. J. E. Fitch. Rev. Fitch is 81 years of age and a year ago took it into his head to out-fast Moses. Holy Writ says that Moses fasted 40 days, and to prove to his congregation that one did not have to be superstitious to believe some of these Old Testament tales, Rev. J. E. Fitch, at the age of 80, fasted fifty days; and instead of losing flesh towards the last part of his fast actually gained in weight. He is as vigorous to-day as he was at 21.

Your Mr. Buel spoke of fasters as cranks and faddists and intimated that your solid citizen would not thus be led astray. Professor Colvin is not a crank but one of our best citizens, being well known both in this country and Europe, and spoken of as the probable president of the Pan-American University to be located in Porto Rico.

Very respectfully,

THOS. F. MURPHY.

210 Merriman Ave.,
ASHEVILLE, N. C., 9/11/10.

MR. UPTON SINCLAIR,
ARDEN, DEL.

DEAR SIR, — After fasting for ten days I went off for ten days. Then on for seventeen days, during which time I got rid of a long list of troubles, except a cough, for which I underwent examination by a specialist. I found I had tuberculosis. The entire upper right lobe of my lung and about half of the left upper lung being affected. Now I am up here making a very rapid recovery. I consider that the fasts I took were the best things that could have happened for me, since they eliminated a bunch of troubles that are nearly always present with tuberculosis, such as indigestion, sore throat, rheumatism, etc. All of these left me, and I never felt better in my life than since fasting. I do not believe that such a rapid recovery as I am making could be possible had I not fasted. Fasting did not cure the tuberculosis, but it gave me an excellent stomach, with which to fight it, and tuberculosis will always give way to a good stomach. I did not know I had tuberculosis when I started fasting, but I now know, since learning more about the disease, that I had the trouble in an active state more than nine months before I fasted. My cough got very tame during the fast and very nearly disappeared, but returned as I increased the amount of food I took after breaking the fast, but at no time did it get as bad as it was previous to the fast. I weighed 172 lbs. in May, when I began my fasting and dropped to 148 lbs., and now weigh 180 lbs. and never felt better in my life. Have but a slight spot of the tuberculosis affection left in my right lung.

While I would not recommend others affected with tuberculosis to fast, I would ask that if you have any letters from consumptives who have fasted I would appreciate a copy.

ROLAND A. WILSON.

NEW ZEALAND, Sept. 10, 1910.

DEAR MR. SINCLAIR, — Your article "The Truth about Fasting" in August *Physical Culture* to hand this week has much interested me. The questions you ask at end of article will, I hope, recive many replies, and give much information regarding the fasting cure. I, personally, can supply a considerable amount of just such information as you require, but the fact that I am a druggist in business precludes the giving of such for publication until drugs and I part company. Let me explain. A little under four years ago I came upon a copy of *Physical Culture*. It interested me and I followed up the reading by subscribing, and obtaining various books — Dewey's, Hazzard's, Carrington's, Desmond's, Eales', Bell's and others. I became quite convinced that about 99 per cent of usual medical treatment was wrong, and, in fact, actually detrimental, and often death-dealing to those who were in search of health. More and more I felt that I was doing a big injustice to those who applied to me for help, and an accessory in bad practice by the dispensing of physician's prescriptions. Yet I know that, like myself, the great bulk of the doctors and chemists were acting innocently and even conscientiously when recommending drugs and practicing the accepted drug and surgical treatments. The belief that drugs cure disease is so deeply rooted in the average human mind, and the teachings in medical and druggists' colleges so universal, and even thorough, that doctors and druggists can hardly be blamed for holding to their mother-loves.

However, I had an open mind, and a desire to hand out a square deal, and decided to make a practical test of the new teachings that had come my way.

I started by carefully selecting my patients — those who I believed had a fair amount of intelligence, and whose ailments had supplied them with a fairly long course of pain, worry and expense. Being a druggist in business, it would have been a very foolish thing for me to have wholly condemned drugs. And that is one reason why I selected chronics for a start — I was able to use the argument that as drugs had had a long and faithful trial, and had proven valueless in curing, a fast of nine or ten days would be, at least, worth a trial. My first case was a lady about thirty-five years of age. Complaint, badly swollen, highly inflamed and ulcerated leg, extending from two inches below knee to one inch above ankle, and more than half way around. She proved a good patient. The leg had been bad with more or less severity for fourteen years, and had been treated by several doctors, druggists, and others. She started on an immediate fast. Within twenty-four hours after fast commenced, the inflammation decreased; by the end of the fourth day it had entirely subsided, and by the end of the eighth day not a vestige of the trouble remained. This fast took place over two years ago — she has held reasonably well to the simple foods I advised, and so far there has been no return of the ailment. Her general health has very considerably improved.

Since then I have treated, perhaps, fifty cases by fasting, and many others by simple dieting. Many complete cures have been effected that ordinary medical methods had entirely failed to benefit. My list comprises many ailments, ranging from one to forty-five years in evidence, while the patients themselves have ranged in age from one year to eighty-five years.

X. ——

HASTINGS, MICH., Sept. 11, 1910.

EDITOR, THE *Cosmopolitan*.

Every reader of your magazine owes you a vote of thanks for the Upton Sinclair article on fasting.

Mr. Sinclair said, "There are three dangers attending the fast." In my case there were four — the danger of being sent to the Insane Asylum.

All my neighbors and relations had the utmost contempt for what they termed "my craziness." But notwithstanding all this, I fasted fourteen days, and stomach trouble, heart trouble, kidney trouble, chronic catarrh, and rheumatism, which for years had made life a burden, are no more. I do not have to tell my friends, at this date, that it was a success, they know it. My family physician has since said that it was probably the best thing I ever did in my life.

I consider myself greatly indebted to you for furnishing me so efficient a remedy, free of cost.

Gratefully yours,

MRS. E. L. RAYMOND.

UPTON SINCLAIR.

DEAR SIR, — Yes, you may use my name in connection with my experience.

As I did not take a complete fast the first time, I began again Sept. 4th, and fasted thirteen days, when natural hunger returned. Had none of the unpleasant experiences of the first fast. Was able to be on my feet and work more than at any time in years.

Chronic rheumatism had caused sinewy swelling of my knee joints, that in turn had caused numbness of the feet and lower limbs, making it impossible for me to be on my feet. What I have suffered with them from jar of people walking across the room, or brushing against them, cannot be told. The first fast removed all the pain and soreness. The last fast has brought them down to normal or nearly so. I am confident that

I shall soon be able to walk any reasonable distance.

You are certainly entitled to a place among the public benefactors of the age for giving to the people the knowledge you had gained by the fast.

Gratefully yours,

MRS. E. L. RAYMOND.

20 Bowdoin St., BOSTON, MASS.
Aug. 1, 1910.

DEAR SIR, — I have just read with much interest your article in *Physical Culture* and am minded to send you a brief account of my experience, which has been in some respects more full than your own. In speaking thus, I refer to the fact that my fasts, though not of so long duration as many reported, were complete in this: that my blood and tissue had cleaned up, my mouth was sweet, tongue moist, and there were plenty of the digestive fluids and a call for good plain wholesome food, which was slowly eaten and perfectly digested, and my appetite was perfectly satisfied with a very moderate amount.

I suffered severely from indigestion and rheumatism, and made up my mind to try the effect of complete abstinence from food till I was better. I was familiar with the writings of Dr. Dewey and was well convinced that he was correct in his views. I was in my office the morning of Jan. 1st, and the bookkeeper remarked as to how ill I looked. Seven days after that (the first seven days of my fast) I was in again, and he spoke of my greatly improved appearance, said

I looked very much better. He did not know nor did I tell him the reason for the improvement. On the 12th day — the first after I had broken the fast — he said I looked much better, which was also true, but when I gave him an explanation of the reason, he would not believe in it at all.

In none of the four fasts which I have taken have I set any time limit or taken it as a stunt at all, but only have been guided by conditions as they developed. In no instance have I failed, and in no case was food a temptation to me until natural hunger returned. It seems to me an error to attempt to gauge the length of the fast. We ought to be governed by nature's direction. A "wise dog" knows when he needs to fast, and fasts till he wants food. It seems to me when we get to that point of wisdom, to know as much as the dog, we will know enough to go by intelligent needs instead of the clock.

My experience is not in accord with the view expressed in your article as regards weakness of stomach and lack of peristalsis after fasting. It is my experience that after a complete fast any plain food desired can be taken without harm. I do not favor imprudence, of course, but I do not think that there is any good reason for being compelled to take fluid foods unless one desires to. My longest fast was nineteen days.

C. D. NORRIS.

39 Rue Singer, PARIS, FRANCE.

DEAR SIR, — I read your article in the May *Cosmopolitan* and was very much impressed with the ideas you advocated. I had for twenty years been troubled with constipation, which caused colds and grippe, besides making me very sluggish. Being a singer and teacher, these things were great handicaps on my work, so after reading your article I decided to try it. I was in Paris studying singing with Oscar Seagle and Jean de Reszke, and of course I needed to be at my very best all the time, but I was n't. I could n't keep from taking cold, which always knocked me out of a week or two of work. So when my teachers went away for their vacation, I decided to start the fast, and on July 31 I did so. Being a coffee "toper," it made it very hard for me to give up my breakfast cup of strong black coffee, but I did it and the first three or four days I nearly lost my mind. Never experienced anything in my life that required so much will power. However, I stuck to it, but I was very hungry and had a splitting headache for four days, after which it got a little better. Then about the fifth day, as my hunger began to leave me, I began to break out as if I had measles — this kept up for five or six days. To add to that, my mouth and throat became inflamed and very sore, and that did n't cure up until about the twelfth day of the fast. I was exceedingly miserable all these days, but I realized how much I needed something of the kind to get the terrible poison out of my system, so I just held on and drank much water, and walked in the sunshine all I could. My tongue had a thick coat on it and I had a terrible bilious taste in my mouth for twelve days. I believed it would take about twenty days to fix me up just right, so I was going ahead when I suddenly decided to make a hurried business trip back to Texas; so on the fourteenth day I sailed from Cherbourg without having broken my fast.

I carried a dozen oranges on board with me to make sure. When I began to breathe the salt air I got hungry, so on the fifteenth day I began to eat oranges and kept it up for a day and a half and then tried to get some milk, but could get none that was good, and most of what I got was of the condensed variety. I did the best I could for four days, when my system rebelled and became clogged up and I took another cold as usual. So I decided not to eat another mouthful on that ship, and I kept the fast up until I got to Ft. Worth. Then I went at the matter according to your instructions, and the results were perfect. I took up oranges for two days, then went on the milk diet for two days, then began on the boiled wheat. The results have been highly satisfactory. Going from a cold climate like Paris into a veritable inferno like Texas in summer made it very hard on me, but the wheat diet did everything for me and gave me unusual strength and vigor even in that hot climate where vigor does n't abound much in hot weather. All my troubles seemed to disappear. I had not sung a tone since I began the first fast in Paris, so I began to practice again, and I never realized such a change in anything. Everything went so easy and all my friends said that they never saw such improvement in a human voice. I have never even desired to taste coffee.

I am living on wheat, nuts, all kinds of fruit and vegetables, and the result is everything you said it would be. I have completed my business in Texas and will start back to Paris to-day. I am preparing myself for the journey this time. I have a large "thermos" bottle which I have filled with wheat and will carry plenty of fruit and nuts.

I thank you very much for your information along the line of health. You have been a great blessing to me, and I am sure you have been also to thousands of others.

ANDREW HEMPHILL.

OMAHA, NEB.

DEAR MR. SINCLAIR, — I was so fascinated with the story of your fast that I immediately made the experiment for myself, abstaining entirely from food of any kind for five days.

I had no particular ailment which seemed to need the fast cure, but felt impelled to do a little investigating on my own account.

I kept a diary in which I recorded each day's experience, including loss in weight, effect of cold bath, amount of exercise taken, etc. Without going into details, I can simply say I was astonished by the results. While in one respect my experience differed from yours, in that the desire for food did not entirely cease at any time, I was surprised to find how easily it could be controlled after the first day. Since the fast I have kept on drinking large quantities of pure water — resulting in a gain in weight of twelve pounds, increased digestive powers and a wonderfully improved appetite.

I am frank to say I was never so pleased with, nor so greatly benefited by anything ever previously extracted from a magazine article.

R. E. WHEELER.

750 PENOBSCOT B'LD'G, DETROIT,
Oct. 19, 1910.

DEAR MR. SINCLAIR, — Complying with your suggestion, will hurriedly and briefly group my experiences through a fast which I took largely because of your persuasive article on that subject. I absorbed the inforation you gave as well as I could, and having been a great sufferer for over twenty years with stomach and bowel troubles, began a fast which I continued for nearly eleven days, adhering scrupulously to the program outlined by you, in so far as I could practically do so, except I took only one bath (tepid) daily before retiring and omitted the enemas after the fifth day. Am fifty-seven years of age, powerfully built and athletic in habit and practice. Normal weight around two hundred pounds, height six feet one and one-half inches. Various causes reduced my weight some four years ago to about one hundred and eighty-five pounds, and almost constant non-assimilation of foods prevented my regaining normal weight. Weight an hour previous to my last lunch prior to the fast, one hundred and eighty-six pounds; lost fourteen pounds during the fast, eight of which fell off me the first three days. My indigestion had for years been accompanied by distressing, persistent constipation. This did not yield until the afternoon of fourth day of fast, when my entire intestinal functions seemed to become normal, and although I had taken no food, solid or liquid, no fruit juices, coffee, tea or milk, absolutely nothing in fast except Detroit River water, hot or cold, as fancy suggested, after the fourth day the bowels inclined to movement at least twice during each twenty-four hours. Lost strength gradually throughout fast, but looked after essentials in my office from six down to three hours the last day. I had no pronounced desire for food from first to last. Tongue remained heavily furred throughout the fast, breath offensive, even to myself. I sat at table at breakfast and evening meals, serving same, but using only a cup or two of hot water as my portion. Voice lost resonancy and timbre, and I finally felt so enervated that I broke the fast — juice of an orange first evening, and of five oranges the second day; of six oranges the third day, during which I also sipped a quart of rich milk, hot. Fourth day ate six oranges, two quarts milk, slice of old bread and about three-fourths pound juicy steak, after which I soon began to eat more than the usual quantity of wholesome food. For over four months had no indigestion, bowels regular and normal.

I am hoping to see my way clear to fast again soon, for am needing a brace physically. . . . I owe you grateful thanks for inciting me to undertake the remedy.

With best wishes for your continued success, usefulness and happiness.

Sincerely,

M. E. HALL.

In my discussion of the question of what to eat, I have referred to the meat diet, and also to the raw-food diet. By way of throwing further light upon the problem, I reprint here two letters, one by a follower of Dr. Salisbury, and the other by a man whom I was instrumental in starting upon raw food. The latter article is reprinted from *Physical Culture*, by courtesy of Mr. Bernarr Macfadden. The reader may find it difficult to understand how two people can have had such apparently contradictory experiences. I myself, however, have no doubt of the literal truth of their statements, for I know dozens of people who are thriving upon each of these diets. It is to me only a further proof of the fact that our knowledge of this subject is as yet in its infancy, and that all one can do is to experiment, and find out what system best agrees with his own organism.

504 West Second St.,
LOS ANGELES, CAL., July 28, 1910.

DEAR SIR, — As you say in the August *Physical Culture* that you would like to hear the experiences of fasters, I will tell you of mine. In 1889–1890 I was very sick with catarrh of the stomach and bowels, which developed into consumption of the bowels accompanied by inflammatory rheumatism. On May 1st, 1890, I went to the office of Dr. James H. Salisbury and treated with him for one year. During the first nine months I ate nothing but Salisbury steaks, beginning with one ounce per meal and increasing gradually as I could assimilate it to one pound per meal, and drank a pint of hot water an hour and a half before meals and at bedtime. Salisbury steak, as you probably know, is beef pulp,—round steak with all fat and fibres removed. I dropped weight rapidly, going from 140 pounds to 90 pounds as this loss was diseased flesh. I then gained as rapidly on beef alone and this was good hard flesh. During the next three months he allowed me a slice of toasted bread at two meals daily in addition to the meat. For the past twenty years I have eaten meat three times a day with other foods, consequently have not needed a physician in that time. I have foolish spells occasionally and indulge in fruit, vegetables and cereals, and destroy the proper ratio, viz: 2/3 of meat to 1/3 of other foods, then I begin to get out of shape and this brings me to my fasting experiences,—about eight of them in the last seventeen years and lasting from five to fifteen days according to the time it took for my tongue to clear off. I find that the more hot water I drink the quicker it clears; during the last fast three years ago I drank one quart every two hours through the day. I got my stomach so clean that the water tasted sweet — this is the test of a clean stomach.

Fasts have benefited me and I recommend them, as few people will live on beef till their blood gets pure; that an exclusive diet of beef *will* make pure blood I saw demonstrated in New York at Dr. Salisbury's by microscopic tests of my own blood and that of others. When you are in this condition you can expose yourself as much as you like without danger of taking cold. If people suffering with stomach and intestinal troubles, Bright's disease, diabetes, rheumatism, sciatica, or tuberculosis, would eat nothing but beef pulp and drink hot water before meals they would be cured in nine cases out of ten, as this was Dr. Salisbury's average of cures when they stuck to the treatment. I acknowledge that one gets rid of a lot of diseased tissue while fasting, but not more rapidly than on the beef diet, and the latter has the advantage that one is making good blood all the time. I consider that you are doing a great work in recommending the fast cure, and agree with you that *Hamburg* steak is not the best food to break a fast with, as it contains 1/4 to 1/3 of fat and "animal fat is a lower form of organization, in fact is often a process of degeneration." I have seen several Salisbury patients have slight bilious attacks from eating over-fat beef, but they quickly recovered by eating leaner beef. Beef pulp is the best thing to eat after a fast as it is absorbed quickly into the circulation and I never saw a patient whose stomach was too weak to digest it in small quantities, well broiled. I believe in dry foods, well masticated, — no slops.

Dr. Salisbury said to me " a man whose food is beef can live in a hole in the ground and be healthy." His last words to me were, " Stick to beef and hot water the rest of your life and nothing but old age will kill you barring accident." I asked him how long he had lived on this diet, he replied, " thirty years." — " Do you expect to die of old age? " " Sure." He died August 23rd, 1905, at the age of eighty-two from the result of an accident. He was a most scientific and successful practitioner; but nearly all physicians, aside from those he cured, called his treatment a farce and a delusion because his teachings if generally followed would put the majority of them out of business. One New York doctor told me while I was on the diet " unless you give up beef and hot water you will not live five years — you will wear your kidneys out." I replied, " you doctors say I am going to die anyway, so I might as well die clean." I immediately increased my hot water from one pint to one quart before each meal and have kept it up ever since. When I began drinking hot water I had a slight kidney and bladder trouble; this has disappeared; the constant flushing has strengthened these organs, — I am now sixty-four.

Cold water before meals is better than none, but is not as good as hot water, as the latter does not chill the stomach or gripe one, and acts as a tonic on the internal organs; is more quickly absored and starts perspiration, causing the skin to share with the kidneys the work of eliminating waste matter. If a person is not very sick he can eat his round steak (after removing the fat) ground without removing the fibre. For a regular Salisbury steak leave the knife loose and clean the grinder frequently.

You have a large contract in trying to force medical men to recognize the fast cure. They even told me, "while we think you are honest, you are mistaken; you did not see Dr. Salisbury perform the cures you think you saw." The Doctor considered me one of his star patients; he said I was as far gone as any man he ever saw cured by the treatment, and that he would rather have three cases of tuberculosis of the lungs than one like mine, my disease being in the last stage.

You can do as you like with this letter. I write simply to strengthen you. Persist, you are on the right track at last. You are no "shallow sensationalist." I like your writings.

Very sincerely,

JAS. Y. ANTHONY.

## THE FRUIT AND NUT DIET

From early childhood until January 9, 1910, or about twenty years in all, I had been a sufferer from asthma, and chronic catarrh in addition. As a child I was sick a great deal of the time, having regular attacks every few weeks, of such little troubles as bilious fevers, chills and la grippe, with pneumonia, typhoid, measles, whooping cough and the like sprinkled in at times. I have taken gallons of castor oil, and pounds of calomel and quinine, I think. I don't believe I ever had more than one cold, but I was never really free of that.

The first attack of asthma came shortly after the disappearance of a severe case of eczema, and from that time on throughout the entire twenty years, I did not pass a single moderately cold night without having at least one, and more often, two and three spasms of asthma during the night. These were relieved temporarily, only after sitting up in bed and inhaling, for several minutes, the smoke from a green powder which I burned for that purpose. Frequently attacks would last continually for three and four days or a week, during which time I was not able to draw a single free breath, and would suffer so intensely that on many occasions I felt as if I was breathing my last. I mention all this for fear some Salisbury followers may doubt that mine was a real genuine case of asthma. In that case, I think I can get satisfactory evidence from our family physician and others who were with me a great deal during that time.

As I grew older, and about the time I went to work for myself, I began to be interested in physical culture methods, and noticed a great improvement by exercising and cutting down my diet, and afterwards adopting the two-meal-a-day plan. However, there was one thing which is strongly emphasized in these methods that did not work with me at the time, but seemed to make the asthma worse; and that was the fresh air idea. I always had better results, and the attacks were less frequent and not so severe, when I closed the windows and doors, and filled the room with the smoke and fumes of the remedy I used. That was due mostly to the narcotic effect of the remedy when breathing the smoke and fumes continually. I mention this for fear some one may suggest that the ultimate permanent relief was brought about simply by breathing fresh air continually when I did begin to open the windows.

During all this time, I ate meat with each meal, or twice daily.

I began to notice that nuts and especially pecans, of which I am particularly fond, and which are quite plentiful in that part of the country in which I live, seemed to have a decidedly bad effect on my asthma, and a greater part of the time I would not touch them on this account. At that time, however, I had the impression that generally prevails among a large majority of people, that nuts or fruits were only good for eating between meals, or as a dessert at the end of a meal, and in addition to the regular food that was eaten; and that was the way I had eaten them.

Mr. Upton Sinclair's first article in the *Physical Culture* magazine on the fruit and nut diet was the first hint I ever had that fruit and nuts eaten alone as a diet had any real substantial food value. From this time on I began experimenting with short fasts of one meal or one day, and also began substituting fruit for some meals, and at the same time cut down my meat eating from twice daily to two or three times a week. I noticed a great improvement in both asthma and catarrh, although I continued having attacks of asthma almost every night, as this was during the winter and most of the nights were quite cold.

After the appearance of his second article, I determined to try this diet out in my own case, hoping to lessen the attacks of asthma at least, never dreaming of the real surprise that was in store for me. I fasted the last two days of December, 1909, and started in January 1st, eating mostly acid fruits, such as lemons, oranges, grape fruit, etc. (This in order to relieve the constipation that I was then, and had been troubled with more or less for the past two or three years.) As a result of the fast, and of what might be termed a partial fast for a few days after, I lost several pounds in weight, which I did not regain until after I had been eating other fruits for several days, such as dates, figs, bananas and apples, also all kinds of nuts, including the much dreaded pecan, which seemed to cause so much trouble before.

On the night of January 8, 1910, I had my last attack of asthma, and have had none since. By that time my bowels were perfectly free, and all traces of constipation gone. The night of the 9th I spent in peaceful, dreamless sleep, my head perfectly clear of any cold or catarrh, enabling me to breathe freely through my nose during sleep, which had never been possible before this.

Although the temperature outside was a little above zero, and stood close around there during the greater part of January and February where I was, two windows in my room were wide open all of the time, and I slept between them; also there was no stove or other heating appliances in the room to warm me on retiring and arising.

I stuck rigidly to the fruit and nuts, living on them alone until the weather began to grow warmer. I then grew so confident, that I gradually lapsed into a general raw-food diet, and later on, to a partly raw and partly cooked diet, but no meat at all, save at times, when it was necessary in order to avoid unpleasant controversies and explanations among people who knew nothing on the subject, and were therefore sceptical, and often inclined to ridicule me.

With the return to cooked foods, came a return of constipation, and with it, traces of the old cold or catarrh. This is one thing I noticed in particular; that when my bowels were moving freely, then and only then was I free of catarrh or cold. I am situated at present where I am away from the influences of kind-and-well-meaning friends and members of my own family, so am living on a raw-food diet entirely, doing heavy gymnasium work every day, also quite a bit of study and other brain work besides, which in all keeps me quite busy most of the day. I am enjoying the best of health in every particular all the while.

H. MITCHELL GODSEY.

## The Rader Case

Mr. L. F. Rader of Olalla, Wash., died at 12.15 P. M., May 11, 1910, at 123½ Broadway North, in the forty-seventh year of his age. Mr. Rader's physical history is one of intermittent suffering. As the result of an accident in childhood in which he was internally injured, his youth and early manhood were filled with a succession of most acute attacks of painful illness. About fifteen years ago he deserted the orthodox means of treatment and turned to what is now known as the natural or drugless method, with the consequence that he experienced the first relief he had ever known. Three years ago he lay ill for three months, and after again submitting to medical treatment he turned to the fast and to me. In fourteen days he was up and about, and in a month he was able to attend to his ordinary business. Since then he had no return of acute symptoms until March 31 of this year, when, after unwonted physical exercise and a heavy meal, he was seized with severe pains in the intestines, which compelled him to take to his bed. His stomach rejected food, and within a week the taking of water brought nausea. I was then called to diagnose the case and to direct treatment. I made the statement at that time to Mrs. Rader that there seemed but little chance for his recovery, but tried the administration of fruit juices and light broths.

The point was soon reached, however, when Mr. Rader refused any sustenance, since it resulted only in nausea and excruciating pain. In the meanwhile the patient came to Seattle, and went to the Hotel Outlook with every symptom showing the relief that is the logical sequence of removing food temporarily from a system struggling to right abnormal conditions. Things progressed smoothly until meddlesome outsiders interfered and caused the city health officials to take cognizance of the fact that a man was " starving " in the hotel. Without warrant Mr. Rader's rooms were entered, and he was confronted by Drs. Bourns and Davidson, who endeavored to persuade him to return to orthodoxy and to the care of the orthodox physicians. Mr. Rader's indignant repudiation is of record, as is also the result of the attempt to declare him insane.

In connection with the latter, after his removal to a quiet, comfortable room in the upper part of the city, an order of the court, obtained in some manner by the health officials, sent the humane officers to the rescue, and the house was watched and guarded while the faithful nurses prevented forcible entry attempted by these servants of the people. The latter even went so far as to raise ladders to the window of Mr. Rader's room, and with display of weapons tried to force the catches in the vain effort to serve the writ which was their excuse. To prevent their seeing the patient and to save him as much as possible from the noisy disturbance, I carried him to the bath and locked the door. I then climbed from one window to another across a court into the next flat in order to call the attorney for the humane society, who took the needful steps that eventually recalled the writ. In the meanwhile Mr. Rader had suffered mentally to such an extent that his life was despaired of for many hours, and he never fully recovered from the nervous shock, which undoubtedly hastened his end. Until the coming of these officers he was able to walk from his room to the bath, but afterwards he continually begged to be protected from outsiders and to be permitted to die, if need be, in peace.

When the death of a patient under my care occurs I am most anxious that no stone should be left unturned to exhibit the cause. In this, my seventh death in four years' practice in Seattle, I find my diagnosis and prognosis completely corroborated. I was assisted in the autopsy by two old-line physicians and by the deputy coroner. The results of the post-mortem examination were as follows:

Mr. Rader's viscera showed the most abnormal characteristics it has been my fortune to observe in years of post-mortem work. The lungs were adherent at every point to the pleural cavity as well as to the diaphragm in places. The heart in fair condition. Stomach dilated and prolapsed. Gall bladder in three distinct pouches, any one of which was the size of the normal sac, and two of these sections were filled with 126 gall stones of one grain to half an ounce in weight; the largest was 3 inches in circumference one way and 4 inches the other way. The small intestines collapsed to the pelvis and midway intussuscepted so that a section of two measured yards occupied but five inches in length; portions of these were of infantile development. The transverse colon lay anterior to the descending colon throughout its extent, while the ascending and descending colon showed infantile size and cartilaginous structure. The sigmoid bend and rectum were of diameter not larger than the adult thumb and in advanced cartilaginous state. The kidneys fair; the liver enlarged and badly congested.

The conditions exhibited were such that the wonder in any mind practised in the care of the human body lies in the thought that nature was able to preserve under these handicaps this man's life until the forty-seventh year. To me this is proof positive that "man does not live by bread alone."

The facts given may easily be verified. Mr. Rader fasted because he had to fast. He could not take food in any sort or in any manner, and his death occurred because of organic disease beyond repair. He was never without water and fruit juices; vegetable broths and prepared foods were given whenever the occasion seemed to present itself, but always with painful consequences. During the month of April he was virtually fasting, although food was supplied as mentioned. It is not at all remarkable in my work to have patients abstain from food for thirty, forty, and fifty days, although by far the greater number do not require this length of time.

Criticized as I have been for my methods, and realizing that the combined efforts of the old schools are aimed at what it eventually means, perhaps a definition may not prove amiss:

Starvation consists in denying food, either by accident or design, to a system clamoring for sustenance.

Fasting consists in intentional abstinence from food by a system non-desirous of sustenance until it is rested, cleansed, and ready for the task of digestion. Food is then supplied.

The conduct of the health and humane officers in the Rader case is not the first instance of their methods of procedure that it has been my fate to experience. In the latter part of January, 1908, I had under my care Mrs. D. D. Whedon, a young married woman in a critical state of health, mother of one child and about to become the mother of another. Officious neighbors complained to the authorities that the child was being subjected to the fasting method and was slowly starving. Without warrant these creatures of authority entered the apartments of Mrs. Whedon, subjected her to a bodily examination against her will and protests, took her child from her by force, and when her husband attempted to regain possession of his daughter, they arrested him for resisting an officer and had him placed in the city jail. I also was charged at this time with practising medicine without a license, an accusation that was quashed on appeal to the superior court.

I rather court an investigation of my work and its results, successful and unsuccessful. Thus far the methods pursued by those antagonistic have been the very ones that have succeeded in informing the world at large that the work is here, that it progresses, else why the furor? It is here to stay and to do what the truth eventually always does — prevail.

The autopsies in each of the several deaths that have occurred in my practice in the city of Seattle have exhibited organic disease, the origin of which lay in the early years of life. In all of these bodies arrested development of one or other of the vital organs was in evidence, and in the majority the injured intestines showed cartilaginous structure and deformation that must have required either violent shock or continued functional disturbance to produce. In view of the fact that these instances cover subjects who had endeavored to follow orthodox methods until orthodoxy proved unavailing, and who then turned to the fast and its accompaniments, I feel perfectly confident in declaring that early drug treatment is responsible for later and fatal disease. Nature had endowed each of these patients with strong vitality; each of them had suffered from severe functional disorder in infancy; each had been drug-drenched.

Broadly speaking, there is no drug that is not a poison, stimulating or paralyzing in result, and in infancy the latter is doubly apparent and appalling. It needs but the parallelism between the effect of an application of a glass of brandy upon an infant and an adult to emphasize this statement. Consider then the consequences of repeated dosings for fevers, colic, colds, and the varied category of infantile disease, and conceive the results upon tender, growing, human bodies. Not one of us but has these sacred relics of the days of powdered dried toads and desiccated cow manure to blame for organs arrested in development or functionally ruined.

The principle embodied in the intelligent application of fasting for the cure of disease is not to be crushed by vilification. The knowledge of it, thanks to strenuous attacks by the medical profession, has been distributed gratis throughout the English-speaking world; and my own part in the work of propaganda has been made more than easy by opposition displayed. I believe that I have a cause to defend, a truth to uphold, a principle for which, if need be, I shall die fighting.

LINDA BURFIELD HAZZARD.

SEATTLE, WASH., May 16, 1910.

## HORACE FLETCHER'S FAST

Dec. 11, 1910.

MR. HORACE FLETCHER,
Care EDITOR OF *Good Health,*
BATTLE CREEK, MICH.

MY DEAR MR. FLETCHER, — It must have been a year and a half ago that we had our talk on the subject of fasting; you promised me that you would investigate it. I have only just seen the copy of the November *Good Health*, and discovered that you carried out your promise. There are some things in connection with your account about which I want to ask you.

You say that you have come to agree with Dr. Kellogg, that autointoxication continues during the fast; and that your reason for this is that at the end of a couple of weeks you found yourself developing weakness, bad breath, coated tongue, etc. You broke your fast because these symptoms grew worse and worse. Now surely if a person is going to give a fair trial to the claims of the fasters, he should follow their instructions, and he should not proceed in opposition to their most important advice. You say that for four days you took no water, and that after that you took only a pint or so a day. In this you violated the leading injunction of every advocate of fasting with whose writings I am acquainted; I have read the books of Bernarr Macfadden, C. C. Haskell, and Dr. L. B. Hazzard, all of whom have treated scores and hundreds of patients by means of the fast, and all of whom are strenuous on the point that one should drink as much water as possible. I myself while fasting have taken at least a glass every hour. I believe that a very great deal of your trouble may have been caused by your procedure in this respect.

Another point which you do not mention is whether or not you took an enema during the fast. This is a very important point. It may very well be true that poisons are excreted into the intestinal tract, and that owing to lack of food they are reabsorbed; if we can aid nature by washing these poisons out at once, can we not overcome this difficulty? May not the reason for the non-success of your fast lie here?

If it be true that the fast leads to constantly increasing autointoxication, how do you account for those phenomena which are summed up in the phrase, "the complete fast"? ·I personally do not advocate the complete fast; I only advocate the investigation of it. I have never taken one, but I have letters from many people who have taken them, and they are in agreement upon the point that there comes a time during the fast when the tongue clears, the breath becomes pure, and hunger manifests itself in unmistakable form. How can this possibly be true if Dr. Kellogg's explanation of the symptoms of fasting is correct? Would it not happen just to the contrary, would not the symptoms of autointoxication increase, until death through poisoning resulted?

Dr. Kellogg's argument is a very plausible one; for many years it sufficed to keep me from trying the experiment of the fast. I know that it has kept many other people. His claim is, in brief, that during the fast the body is living off its own tissue; that we are therefore meat-eaters, and even cannibals, while fasting. We are living on a kind of food which is over-rich in proteid, and which generates excessive quantities of uric acid, indican, etc. This, as I say, sounds plausible, but I found by actual experiment that the facts do not work out according to the theory. I myself have taken a week's fast recently, with perfect success. During this time I had not one particle of weakness or trouble of any sort. Perhaps it may be that my body was excreting undue amounts of uric acid and indican, but I did not know it, and it did me no harm so far as I could discover. I am much less afraid of the consequences of living from my own body tissue, since I have tried for myself the experiment of living on the tissues of other animals.

I am trying to get at the truth about these questions, and I know that you are trying to do it also. For three years I did myself incalculable harm by accepting blindly statements that meat was the prime cause of autointoxication, together with other high proteid food. I lived on starches and sugars, grew pale and thin and chilly, and, as I was accustomed to phrase it, was never more than fifteen minutes ahead of a headache. I can give myself a headache at any time at present by two or three days of eating rice, potatoes, white flour, and sugar. Apparently I cannot give it to myself by eating any possible quantity of broiled lean beef. So far as I can make out, beef is the one article of diet which never does me any harm, no matter how much of it I eat. The same thing is true, apparently, with my little boy.

I wish you would tell me what you think about all this. I wish that I could induce you to try the experiment of fasting again with the use of the enema and the copious water drinking. Still more do I wish that you could be induced to try it with some people who need it — some people who are desperately ill, and who have not been able to get well by following the low proteid diet.

Sincerely,

UPTON SINCLAIR.

NORWICH, CONN., U. S. A.
Dec. 23, 1910.

MY DEAR MR. SINCLAIR, — Your valued favor of the 14th inst. received enclosing copy of your letter to Horace Fletcher. I have read your letter to Mr. Fletcher with much interest, and I have also read Mr. Fletcher's letter to Dr. Kellogg in *Good Health.*

I am so crowded with work that I cannot take the time to write you on this subject of Fasting as I would like. I have had nearly seventeen years' experience studying and practising the "no-breakfast plan and fasting for the cure of disease." I have followed the no-breakfast plan all that time without a single break, and I know it has been of exceedingly great value to me. It has also been my privilege and pleasure to advise in thousands of cases covering nearly all forms of disease, and where the Law of Fasting has been followed faithfully, there have always been splendid results.

Aside from the omission of the breakfast, I have fasted a great many times from one day to four weeks, and always the results have been beneficial. This could not have been the case if Dr. Kellogg's contention is correct, that autointoxication continues and increases during a fast. If his idea is correct on this point, instead of one improving and at last overcoming the disease entirely, there would not only be a continuation of the disease but an increase, and death would naturally result. Should autointoxication continue and increase while one is fasting, the time would not come when the tongue would be clean and natural hunger manifest itself. On the contrary, there would be an increase of the coating on the tongue until death finally resulted.

I think if Mr. Fletcher had continued his fast until his tongue had become clean, which certainly would be the case, he would have written a very different letter. In the case of Mrs. Tarbox, whose letter I enclose, on the thirty-seventh day of her fast, her tongue was perfectly clean and she had natural hunger, and she was well on the way to recovery from the terrible cancerous growth and condition in which I found her. Since Mrs. Tarbox' cure, I have had several other cases of cancer cured through fasting. You will note the case of Mrs. Hobson, copy of whose letter I enclose, and the case of Mr. Davis is another very interesting case as well as that of Mrs. Osborne. These persons would not have been cured if auto-intoxication had been going on and increasing.

Dr. Dewey's contention I know to be true, that during a fast the heart, lungs, and brain are supported by the predigested food stored up in the body. These organs take the nourishment and not the poison, for during a fast the eliminating organs work to the very limit to force the poison out of every cell of the body, so that during a fast all the poison in the body is growing less every hour, and when it is all eliminated natural hunger manifests itself, the tongue is clean, and the patient is ready to build up and have a clean physical organism. The use of the enema is exceedingly important during a fast. I believe that it hastens the cure at least twenty-five per cent, and perhaps more than that.

Mr. Fletcher's own letter is to my mind a refutation to Dr. Kellogg's claim as to the continuation and increase of autointoxication, for he tells the benefits that he has received during his fast of seventeen days, and those benefits would have been greatly increased if he had continued the fast until his tongue was clean. His sense of taste had become so refined by the fast that his food was more delicious than ever before, which showed that the refining process had been going on all through his body. Another benefit that he mentions is the lessening of his desire for sugar, that he is satisfied with the sugar sweet that is in the food itself, which is so much more healthful than the cane sugar. Another thing that he speaks of is the reduction in his weight, which he needed. I sincerely hope that Mr. Fletcher will fast again, and make it a complete fast, for I think he will have a very different story to tell from what he tells in this letter.

CHARLES COURTNEY HASKELL.

Dec. 28, 1910.

DEAR MR. SINCLAIR, — I have your letter of the 14th inst. and its enclosures.

To those who have carefully and scientifically undergone or advised the fast, the cause of the symptoms that Dr. Kellogg and all of the rest of us recognize as indicating self-poisoning, is readily discovered to lie in the inability of the organs of elimination to promptly convey from the body the products of food supplied in excess of digestion. It is a conclusion that cannot be escaped that, when the refuse from broken-down tissue and from food ingested beyond the needs of the body is discharged into the intestines, and when means of removal are not at hand, re-absorption at once begins and continues until the canal is cleansed. Self-poisoning, autointoxication, ensues, and all of its symptoms were emphatically shown in the fast of seventeen days that Mr. Fletcher essayed. These results are also often observed when feeding is in progress, and in this connection I refer to an article written by Dr. Kellogg for *Good Health* in the summer of 1908. In it he says, "The writer's observations, extending over a considerable number of years, have brought him to the conclusion that the cases which are benefited by fasting are practically without exception cases of autointoxication, generally cases of intestinal autointoxication, though perhaps also including some cases of metabolic autointoxication." It seems to me that the Doctor has not made it quite clear just why, if the fast is the certain producer of the condition, he recommends it for the cure of the condition. Perhaps "similia similibus" or "the hair of the dog theory" is implanted in the Doctor's ego.

As we review the situation, covering in origin thousands and thousands of years of wrong living, the facts are patent. The processes of digestion and assimilation as functions have long since lost natural expression. Drugs and heredity have created in them an inability to cope with their work without assistance, and have in many instances caused a positive cessation of normal action.

Dr. Kellogg would have us accept his dictum that the cause of loss of weight during the fast is to be found in the impoverished state of the blood, and in the fact that, food being denied, no upbuilding of tissue can occur. Can he explain in this manner the wasting of tissue in illness when food is regularly supplied? It should be readily understood that, in either instance, the process of elimination of decomposed excess food has at last become the predominant function of the diseased system. Fasting is the voluntary act that permits rapid accomplishment of the result; and disease itself is but Nature's attempt to cleanse and purify by means of elimination. The longer this thought is dwelt upon, and the more its details are verified by experiment, the stronger becomes the conviction that we are facing the truth of the matter.

When coated tongue, foul breath, and vertigo appear, whether feeding or fasting, hunger is absent. It must have disappeared many days before these signs became acute, although Nature's warnings did not fail of display. The sensation of hunger, the desire for food for the purpose of restoring cell life, is the human body's greatest natural safeguard. A sentinel of lower rank is the sense of taste, which, however, like other outposts, often becomes debauched and valueless. But hunger never can be turned from its protecting task, and it cannot be stimulated into action. Hunger is the one natural function that is incorruptible, for once abused it withdraws. Its deceptive counterpart, appetite, is the product of taste-stimulation, and, as Mr. Fletcher says, takes upon itself the guise of habit. Or, as expressed in the text of my book, "Appetite is craving; Hunger is desire. Craving is never satisfied; but Desire is relieved when Want is supplied. Eating without Hunger or pandering to Appetite at the expense of Digestion makes Disease inevitable."

Had real normal hunger been present when Mr. Fletcher broke his fast, the demand for food would have been so great and so insistent that no denial would have been tolerated. Mr. Fletcher states that he did not want food until he had tasted it, — a clear case of taste-stimulation or appetite. Even this was momentary and was but the expiring flame of taste relish left after seventeen days free from the progressive accumulation of excess food. Despite his care in the selection and the mastication of his food, Mr. Fletcher must still have continually eaten without hunger, and must, as a result, have stored within his system an unusual amount of material beyond the needs of his body. Had this not been true, he would not have exhibited the coated tongue, foul breath, and vertigo. Hunger would have been ever present, and it would have been impossible for him to fast.

My only comment upon the neglect of the enema that seems to have occurred in the conduct of Mr. Fletcher's fast is that it was a most vital error. The enema is absolutely necessary. The question of diet also need not be discussed, for experience shows that the feeding of the body is a matter of individual requirement. If normal physical balance be ever reached, fixed laws to govern the diet problem could be formulated. In its present state, argument resolves itself into mere utterances of individual opinion and prejudice.

Faithfully yours,

LINDA BURFIELD HAZZARD.